I0768755

COLD SUMMER BLUES

KAREN L ROSE

Copyright © 2024 Karen L Rose

All rights reserved.

No part of this book may be reproduced or used in any manner without written permission of the copyright owner except for the use of quotations in a book review.

Cover and interior layout by Blue Pen

ISBN: 979-8-9908862-3-0 (hardcover)
ISBN: 979-8-9908862-4-7 (paperback)
ISBN: 979-8-9908862-5-4 (ebook)

Cindy – I hear your beautiful laughter; I see your enormous smile, and I know you are in your happy place! Enjoy shopping in all the heavenly stores and give a huge hug to everyone we know!

CHAPTER 1

Cindy woke up by herself, early as usual, and tied up her hair into a ponytail. Her bangs had finally grown long enough so that she no longer had the annoying habit of pushing them off her forehead. She quietly rolled off the lower bunk bed and gently slipped on her faded overalls. They still had damp grass stains on the knees from yesterday, but they were soft and worn in – just how she liked them. Her Livingston Meadows Tee shirt was already on since she slept in it – again – so it was easy to pull up the overall straps. A pair of socks lay on the floor from last night – and that was a no-brainer to grab. The boots were still not totally broken in, but very comfortable now that her blisters had morphed into hard calluses. And finally, her prized possession – an authentic cowboy hat. Her mother's last gift to her before they both said their tearful goodbyes.

Cindy opened the door from her bunk slowly. She did not want to disturb the other counselors. She closed the door gently and took a deep cleansing breath. Walking over to the stables, Cindy hummed her favorite Taylor Swift song. She looked up at the blue sky dotted with puffy clouds and smiled. How could a day so beautiful ever have an ugly ending? The sun was barely poking through the low-hanging clouds in a failed attempt to light up the stables. The grass was wet from last night's incredibly loud thunderstorm but the dirt inside the horse arena was dry except for a few spots that were mostly clumpy with soggy patches on the edges.

Cindy breathed in the mixed aromas of horses and dirt and for no reason at all she twirled. Cindy laughed out loud and then immediately felt guilty for feeling so happy. She caught herself, stopped, and stared up at the clouds. I should not be so happy, she thought. With a wrinkled brow and pouty lips, Cindy trudged slowly toward the large wooden barn.

Cindy loved the barn. She slid open the large wooden barn door to find the ten horses happily grazing in each of their stalls. The smells inside the stalls were different from the outside arena and Cindy embraced their differences from the acrid odor of urine to the sweet musty scents of hay and woodchips to the earthy fragrance of the numerous leather saddles hanging on their pegs at the edge of the office.

There were five stalls on each side and Cindy had memorized each horse's names and their breed. Cindy loved to walk the horses in at night and then muck out their stalls in the morning. She was learning a whole new language from mucking to bit to forelock and leader and tack to name a few. She loved it. She embraced this new world like a newborn baby, and she never felt anxious, nervous, or scared around the horses.

Cindy went to the first stall on the left. She was a Palomino, a golden coat with a beautiful white tail. The name tag on the outside door to the stall said her name was Ariel, and she was 15 hands high. Cindy was so proud when she learned what that meant. "How can you say a horse is tall by its hands?" she asked Billy, the camp director.

Billy was in his late 50's, about 6'4" with the same light colorings as Ariel but she could tell he must have been a tow-head as a child. His nickname was 'the wolf' but Cindy was too afraid to ask anyone how he acquired that name.

"Well," began Billy slowly knowing he had explained this a million times over but loved the telling of it. "You see, a hand equals about four inches so you measure a horse from the ground all the way to the top of its withers."

Cindy scrunched her eyelids close together as though she were trying to understand what a wither was. Or was he saying weather or whether? She was quite confused. Billy observed her facial features right away and smiled.

"Come here a sec, Cindy." Billy carefully took Cindy by the hand and brought her over to Ariel. He placed Cindy's hand on top of the highest point on Ariel's back right where it meets the neck. "See this?" he asked carefully, "this part is called the horse's withers. Back in the day, well, people just didn't have rulers or yardsticks like we have now, so they just used their hands."

"Billy?" Cindy looked up into the most intense blue eyes she had ever seen. "How long have you been around horses?" she asked.

"Well, little lady," Billy loved to go into his cowboy twang routine, "I 'spect I've been around horses bout all my life. You see, my momma and my daddy lived on a farm out west and we just grew everything we ate, and I rode my horse bout every day.

"Got to the time when I was so busy riding my horse all around the county that people would ask me to help them with their horses. You know, like helping with the grooming and the mucking of the stalls and such. It was mostly farmers who were too busy doing their farming to take care of their horses and their other farm animals, especially if they didn't have enough children to do the chores."

"Wow," exclaimed Cindy. "I wish I did that all day instead of going to school and doing homework."

Billy turned Cindy's hand over, so her palm was facing up. He traced his finger from one side of her hand to the other edge of her palm. Then he took her hand and stuck it on the ground and slowly showed her how to measure the horse using the palm of her hand from the ground up to the withers.

"Now, keep in mind, that an adult male is usually doing the measuring of a horse and the palm of his hand is a might larger than yours. Wouldn't you say?"

Cindy nodded in agreement, totally fascinated by what she was learning.

"So how many hands is Ariel, for real?"

"Well, watch me now and I'll show you." Billy dropped Cindy's hand and started measuring with the palm of his hands.

When he got to the withers, he looked at Cindy and she quickly blurted out, "Fifteen! I counted fifteen! So Ariel is fifteen hands high! Right?"

"You got it, my friend. Hold your hands up high so I can do the high five on you!"

• • •

"Hold up your hands, everyone, if you have made definite plans for this summer," asked Neva. She looked around her group, which used to be her dozen, but now included Riley who seemed to emerge as an honorary member recently.

Cindy looked around the circle at her friends. She called them her friends after being with them the entire year. They talked together, laughed together, and sometimes there were tears. Together they joined a close-knit group and most significantly they knew they were directly responsible for bringing back their beloved teacher and mentor, Carl DeWitt.

"That's totally awesome," added Carl. "I am so excited to hear about your summer plans. Now before we leave for the summer…oh, my goodness, this really is our last meeting for the year! All of you are, well, words alone cannot describe what this year has been for me and especially because of all of you.

Yes, you saved me and I cannot thank you enough. I will be forever grateful to each and every one of you!!

"But for right now, before we have our celebration party. Yes, and a huge thanks to Miss Riley for baking all the goodies we are about to consume, but before we do that, I want you to write one last time in your notebooks for Mrs. Waverly and me what your summer plans are and what you hope to gain by these summer plans. Now I know some of you are working, but I don't want you to just say you want to earn money. Sure, that's important, especially if you're like Lucas and are saving up for that Mustang, but besides the money that you will be rolling in by the end of the summer, what are your goals? Personal? Educational? Traveling? Reading? Writing? You name it. Remember…there are no wrong answers! No go ahead, get writing while Mrs. Waverly and I set up the snacks!"

Cindy looked around the circle seeing how quickly everyone was writing. Tommy was speed writing, Jilly was writing and looking up, and writing and looking up; Whitney and Sofia were both humming as they were writing. And the others, including Riley, were busy on task. Only me thought Cindy. What do I write about? Watch my mother inject chemo every week? Watch her hair fall out every day? See her lose so much weight I will barely recognize her? Cindy was holding back tears. She refused to have a melt down now after she felt she had progressed so much this year.

Neva's eyes shifted over to Cindy and noticed immediately that she wasn't writing. Neva gave Carl that knowing tacit look and walked quietly to Cindy. "Cindy, let's go out in the hall for a sec, okay?"

Cindy nodded and slowly pushed her chair away from the desk. She followed Neva like a young puppy, head bowed and shoulders slumped.

Neva took Cindy by the hand and said softly, "Let's go for a walk, shall we?"

Cindy sniffed and wiped her nose with the back of her hands and walked alongside Neva. They were quiet for a long while. Finally, Neva said gently, "Cindy, I know you're going through a lot with your mom right now. I've spoken with her. I know that Riley's parents have been letting you stay there for the last few months. It's a huge adjustment. Tell me, what are you thinking right now?"

Cindy didn't respond at first. How could she tell Mrs. Waverly everything that was on her mind? How long could she live with Riley? Afterall, Riley had her own life and that did not include taking in a temporary sister. She was sure Riley had her summer plans. And Cindy had… Cindy had…

"I have nothing for my summer plans!" Cindy suddenly burst out. "How can I go anywhere? How can I do anything? How can I leave my mother when she…when she…oh, God, what if she doesn't live through the summer? What do I do then?"

Neva took her time answering. She placed her arm around Cindy's quivering shoulders. The sheer strength of Neva's firm arm pressed on Cindy's shoulders seemed to help Cindy from shaking.

"Cindy," began Neva, "do you remember when you wrote in your notebook that you wanted more than anything else in the world to work around horses?"

"Sure, "Cindy replied as she breathed in and out forcing herself not to have a full-blown anxiety attack right there in the hallway. "But don't they call that a pipe dream? I mean, for me, Mrs. Waverly, how would it ever be possible for me to do that? Besides, I need to be around my mom all the time right now. She's really hurting, and she needs me. And, well, I need her."

"Cindy," Neva whispered, "Your mom is going into a special housing for treatment. She won't be at home. You can't live at home alone and the Maddox's will gladly let you live with them for as long as you need to, but..." Neva paused. She stopped walking and facing Cindy looked her squarely in the eyes.

"What if I told you that I could arrange for you to stay at a very special horse farm in the country that specializes in working with kids who have special needs? Would you be interested in working there? It would mean working with other kids and not playing with horses, but more importantly, doing whatever the director of this summer camp needs you to do. Could you do this?"

Cindy's eyes widened so big she thought her eyes would pop like a balloon.

"Are you serious, Mrs. Waverly? Like for real serious? Not fooling me like this is a baby camp you're sending me away to?"

Neva laughed. "No, Honey. I have a very special friend. His name is Billy Tydings. We went to school together many years ago, and his dream was to build a horse farm for kids with special needs who would live at his horse farm during the summer and experience life with horses. He grew up with horses and his sister, well, she has passed on now, but she had special needs. And when Billy would let her ride his horse, he saw what that did for her. How it improved her self-confidence and how it made her laugh. Oh, he loved to tell me how she giggled and chuckled when she rode.

"Anyway, I'm going on here. Let me give him a call and see if he will hire you to be one of his counselors. You are certainly old enough to be a counselor for the kids there and you will love it! I know you will. And you can be in touch with your mom as often as you like."

Cindy beamed. "Oh, Mrs. Waverly, you are the best!" And Cindy reached over and hugged her tight. "Okay, I think I can go back now and finish writing in my journal. Oh, boy, I can't wait to tell my mom and Riley and her parents, too!"

CHAPTER 2

Beverly sat in the hard chair, her back rigid, straight, and inflexible as her mood. She stared at the walls. There were three posters on the stark white walls. One depicted rolling oceans with pockets of deep aqua crashing next to exploding waves of emerald green. The other poster was wrinkled and torn at one edge as it hung limply from the wall. Beverly scoffed at the vision of the deep forest filled with variegated leaves that appeared to be waving at her. She observed a few furry animals that were too blurry to identify. The last poster seemed new and crisp as it seemed glued to the wall. It was a wide angle that depicted a sunrise on one end and a sunset on the other. Beverly snorted out loud as if her nose could shed her disgust at having to sit there.

Beverly's eyes shifted over to the large desk, planted near the window that was sealed shut with soft sky-blue gauzy shades. The shades were sagging, and dust filled and so flimsy that even the most violent individual could not commit suicide with them no matter how desperate they might have been. Beverly closed her eyes as though in prayer waiting for her doctor to enter the room. Even with her eyes closed, Beverly sensed Dr. Carter's entry. He was not a quiet man. She could hear him shuffling his feet as he approached the desk. She knew he would be unbuttoning his jacket, and tugging at his pants before sitting down. Finally, Beverly opened her eyes and stared at Dr. Carter now comfortably seated at his desk. The large mahogany desk was void of anything personal; a laptop sat in the middle closed tight. Seemed symbolic of her mood.

"So, Mrs. Winewrought, how are we today?"

Beverly's beady dark eyes pierced into the soul of her psychiatrist. If looks could implement harm, this poor excuse of a doctor would be dripping in blood.

"We," blurted Beverly," are not talking today. Or any day. But since you included yourself in the question at hand, why don't *we* go on with the conversation?"

Dr. Ethan Carter smiled, his large front yellow coffee-stained teeth biting into his bottom lip till they turned pale from the pressure. Probably his nervous habit Beverly decided. Beverly glanced at Dr. Carter's hands that were clasped together on the desk as though he was forcing himself not to take any notes. She always studied them whenever they were meeting. His hands were huge, calloused, and gnarly. She wondered what he did outside of his work that caused the callouses. Not that she gave a damned hoot about him, but imagining his hobbies or his other extracurricular activities helped pass the time away since Beverly refused to give in to his psycho mumbo jumbo talk he tried to trick her with each time. She chuckled to herself. Thank God he didn't become an OBGYN she thought maliciously. Beverly's eyes rolled up to stare into Dr. Carter's dark blue eyes. There were flecks of silver in them, she noticed. The same kind of silver flecks in his bush eyebrows. Why do men get away with such thick, ugly bushy eyebrows she mused. I could never face myself if I had to sport those every day!

Dr. Carter broke her train of thought. "So, Beverly, to continue with our conversation as you requested, I was thinking about decreasing your dosage of nortriptyline. I think in these past few months that you have been here with us your mood has stabilized, and I am hoping we can begin some discussions that will help you understand the events of that day in school."

Beverly shifted in her seat. Every time this doctor brought up that day in school, Beverly got nauseous and wanted to throw up. She leaned forward and her gag reflex took over. Dr. Carter jumped out of his seat and grabbed his trash can and quickly placed it at Beverly's feet.

The morning breakfast had suddenly turned sour in her stomach, and she heaved violently. Beverly made a futile attempt to aim for the trash can, but her brain only saw red waves rushing in front of her forcing her to lean to the left of the sanitary white trash bag. Her scrambled eggs and toast had morphed into a vile mucous green mixture which gushed out of her mouth and splashed in large clumps onto Dr. Carter's beige rug.

Dr. Carter's dark elderberry eyes widened at the sight, and he immediately ran out of his office shouting for his secretary. Lillian O'Neal, an older woman who was counting her days till retirement, rushed into his office to find Beverly leaning back in her chair smiling, ignoring the gobs of vomit still clinging to her chin.

Lillian stared open-mouthed at the clownish spectacle in front of her. She did not like Beverly. She knew she wasn't supposed to judge the patients who resided in this facility, but Lillian had never met a more evil, obnoxious, and calculating woman. And staring at her now Lillian only wanted to curse at her for her egregious and selfish behaviors.

Beverly looked at Lillian and laughed. She stood up, stepped into the slimy mess on the rug, and slithered over to Lillian. Beverly let her face come close enough to Lillian so that her noxious breath was causing Lillian to gag. Lillian's gentle green eyes turned watery at the nearness of Beverly and she turned her head away to breathe.

Beverly snickered. She hated Lillian. Lillian was beloved by every damn person in this rotting hell hole I'm in thought Beverly. With her God-like white hair, her petite shape, and her caring attitude, Beverly was glad she threw up and felt like doing it all over again.

Instead, Beverly took a slow deep breath, let it out onto Lillian's pale face, and hissed, with spittle spewing forth, "I don't feel well. I'm going back to my room now. Tell Dr. C. I'll see him tomorrow. Maybe." And with that, she sidestepped a shaking Lillian and left the room.

CHAPTER 3

Lucas finished packing his sports bag. He brushed his hands through his hair and stared at his room. It looked like it always did, but there was something out of sync for him. His blue eyes darkened, and he squinted as he surveyed the walls.

"This room is my childhood," he spoke to the walls, his arms waving back and forth, his voice raspy and tight. "You stood there and watched me grow up. You didn't help me when I needed your help," he continued. "And now, before I leave, well, you all got to go. I'm done with you. Forever."

Lucas, quietly, determinedly, pulled down each poster from his wall. Down came John Elway, his father's all-time favorite football player. Down came 98 Degrees. Lucas ripped Christina Aguilera so hard that pieces of the paint floated off the wall and landed on his dark blue carpet.

"It's time for a change," Lucas muttered. Lucas's eyes shifted to his nightstand, and he focused on a picture of him in his elementary boys' club football uniform proudly standing next to his dad. His father, Angelo, had his arm around Lucas's shoulder, and he was holding a football in his other hand. Lucas had a smile as wide as the football field.

"Proud? Happy? Excited to have you next to me?" Lucas picked up the framed picture and held it in his hands, memories flooding back to him like a tsunami that he couldn't escape and his breath caught and his throat tightened.

"You are a son of a bitch, Dad," Lucas choked out the words. "And I will hate you forever." His eyes filled with tears and even though he was determined not to cry over the loss of this man, he couldn't help it. "I'm not crying because I love you," he said to the picture, "I'm crying because you took something away from me and I will never, ever forgive you."

Lucas gripped the picture as though he was strangling a memory, and then he chucked it into his trash can. The glass shattered into little pieces, each sliver tearing away pieces of his heart, leaving gaping holes that would only grow thick scars over the damaged injury.

Lucas grabbed his gym bag, his school sweatshirt, and his football gear, and closing the door behind him felt as if a great weight had been lifted. That is until he walked into the kitchen. His mother had left a letter addressed to him on the kitchen table, She was still at work, but the letter must have arrived in yesterday's mail. The handwriting on the envelope looked familiar. Too familiar. It was from his father. There was no return address.

Lucas dropped all his gear on the kitchen floor and sat down at the table. He was having trouble breathing and Lucas knew from Miss Anna that he was at the beginning of an anxiety attack. He never had those stupid things before, but ever since that night, well, he didn't like to admit it, but he had them more often than he liked to tell anyone. He had been sharing them with Miss Anna and she was giving him some steps on how to control the rapid heartbeats, the short breaths that made him feel like he was suffocating, and the cold sweat that enveloped his body leaving a shimmering tell-tale sign for all the world to see he was in crisis.

"Okay, man," he murmured to himself, "Breathe in, breathe out, let the heart rate go back to normal." Lucas held the envelope in his hand as he spoke his steps out loud. "You can do this," he urged himself. "It's just a letter. It's just something that he wrote. Probably some bull shit that he wants me to know."

Lucas squeezed the envelope tightly while staring out the kitchen window. He was focusing on the large Dogwood tree that stood right outside the kitchen. He closed his eyes. No, be real, he squeezed his eyes shut and then he opened them and stared at the tree again. He counted two cardinals on the branches and one woodpecker that was going to town on the bark.

The focus was working. He could feel his heartbeat slowing back to normal, his hands less clammy and he no longer felt the cold sweat dripping down his back. Lucas turned the envelope over and over in his hands. He tried to read the city on the postmark, but it had blurred so he could not tell where the letter came from.

"I don't even know where you are. I don't care, either. You can rot in hell for all I care." But the letter sat in his hands and Lucas knew he had to open it. He didn't want to, but he knew if he didn't read the letter he would never be able to concentrate at football practice.

"This is stupid," he mumbled. "Okay, Dad, I'll read your goddamn letter but it's not gonna make a difference with me. Not now. Not ever."

Lucas tore open the seal. He took the folded letter out and crumbled the envelope on the table. His fingers were shaking as he took apart the trifold and began reading:

Dear Son, (can I still call you that?)

Lucas, I don't know where to begin. I don't know how to begin. All I know is that I hurt you, son. I hurt you bad and I'm guessing you never want to see me again. Never want to talk to me again.

Lucas, I'm getting help. My therapist told me that I needed to reach out to you. To take baby steps with some sort of connection with you.

I know what I did to you was wrong. I know it from the bottom of my heart, but I don't know how to fix it. I don't know how to fix us. Or if that is even possible.

I miss you so much. I am all alone. Every day I wake up and realize that my life sucks. I lost the only thing I ever loved — you, my boy. You were my life.

I know your mother and I will never be together again. She made that very clear when she sent the divorce papers. She mentioned that she was married to someone, but she won't tell me who. I don't even know how they met.

I hope you like this man. I hope he is good to you. Every time I think of you calling him dad, my heart aches. Maybe you could call him something else? Maybe? I don't know.

I don't get any news where I am staying. They do not let me watch television or read newspapers. At least now yet. But I think of you every day and hope you are doing okay.

How is football? Do you have a girlfriend? Is school going okay? Do you like your teachers? What are

you doing over the summer vacation? Will you get a job or will you
just focus on prepping for football?
Do you like your coaches?

Am I asking too many questions? I
guess I am starved for information
about you.

Okay, I'll let you go. I hope you get
this letter. I hope you don't tear it
up or burn it or something.

Maybe one day you'll write to me
and let me know how you are doing.

For now, Lucas, please know how
very sorry I am for all the hurt I
put on you. I was wrong. I was so
wrong. Maybe I'm just a sick man
and they should throw away the
key.

I only hope someday in the future
you'll be able to accept my sincere
apology.

I will forever be your loving dad.

Xxxxxxoooooo

Lucas wiped the tears away from his swollen eyes. It did
not take him long to let the content of the letter sink in.
Lucas jumped up from the kitchen table, his hand squeezing the letter tightly. He shouted to the window scaring

all of the wildlife in the backyard enjoying the nuts on the birdfeeders, "You disgust me! I hate you! Nothing you say will ever make me change my feelings for you!" And with that, Lucas balled up the letter and threw it in the corner of the kitchen, marched over to where he had dropped his belongings, scooped up his gear, and pounded out the door.

CHAPTER 4

Max should have been suited up for football practice and present at the field ready to participate in the drills at that exact moment, but instead, he was relaxing on the large purple and white flowered duvet that was carelessly thrown on Sofia's bed. The room was swathed in purple light floating in from the deep plum curtains hanging on Sofia's windows. Max felt like he was climbing in his grandmother's lilac bush in full bloom season between the sweet scents of Sofia's perfumed candles and her Potpourri bowl filled with lavender and ivory blossoms.

"Why do girls have so many posters on the wall?" he asked inquisitively. Max's deep brown eyes squinted as he scanned the walls looking at Sofia's eclectic collection from Justin Bieber to Timothy Chalamet to Harry Stiles and Olivia Rodrigo. Why did she have Andrew Garfield next to Jennifer Lopez and then Nirvana thrown in as well?

"Uhhh," asked Max, his fingers forming tight little dred

locks with his high Afro, "Who the hell is that one poster over there?"

Sofia was busy at her computer on her desk. She didn't look up; her head was bent in serious mode with whatever she was focused on. "Hmmmm?" she replied.

"The one that has a signature on the bottom. It looks like." Max sat up, bouncing on the bed as he tried to read the cursive signature. "Damn, I can't read cursive," he mumbled. "Ahh, it looks like David Cassidy or some old guy from the dinosaur days."

"Oh," Sofia responded mindlessly, fingers flying on her keyboard. "That's David Cassidy. He is definitely OG, but my grandma made me put him up there. She said he was her teen idol and if I was going to mess up my walls, then she told my mom I had to include her guy just to make her smile."

Sofia looked over at Max, her fingers still perched on her keyboard.

"What are you working on?" he asked Sofia. Sofia did not answer him. Instead, she flipped back her long dark auburn hair that she had been growing all year long. She hated the short haircut her mother had made her get right before she started high school, and she promised herself she would never allow her mother to give her health or beauty tips ever again.

Max could not stop staring at Sofia. Her full pouty lips produced electric currents that surged through his body, and he did not know how to stop these new sensations. He thought of Sofia every morning, every afternoon, and especially every night before he closed his eyes. His body was making him do things he was not accustomed to doing and he blamed it all on Sofia. But he could not stop himself no matter how many times he tried. And he should have been at football. He knew that. He knew the guys were going to tease him. And he knew the coach was going to punish him with extra laps and God knew what else. But it was worth it. It was all worth it if only…

Sofia sighed. Max didn't want to know what she was doing. He had been staring at her for the past thirty minutes and she was trying so hard to concentrate on filling out a job application. She wanted to work and earn money this summer and Max kept showing up at her doorstep every day. She was sure he had football practice. She knew Lucas and Tommy and Jáquan and Mateo were already at practice. She saw it on their social media page.

Before today, Max would come by her house, see her, talk for a little while, and then leave to go to practice, but not this morning.

"Say, Max," started Sofia. "Shouldn't you be at practice already? I mean the guys are there. I saw it on their page. And isn't there a scrimmage this Friday? What are you telling the coach? Like, is he okay with you not showing up?"

Max rolled up on the bed and adjusted his pants. Without thinking, he grabbed one of Sofia's lavender (of course) pillows and placed it on his lap, embarrassed by his actions but hoping Sofia would not notice.

Sofia was confused. "Max? What's going on with you? I mean, I like that you come over to see me, but I don't know, you're acting weird and you're not doing a whole lot of talking. Actually, you're doing a whole lot of staring!"

Max rubbed his face and closed his eyes looking for the words that could explain his feelings. He slid off the bed, the pillow landing softly on the floor. He walked over to Sofia and deliberately put his arms around her pulling her up from her chair. He wanted her body to melt into his and he locked his eyes on her face memorizing her chocolate eyes, her narrow small nose, and her thick arched eyebrows that were now rising even higher.

Sofia felt uncomfortable. She and Max had kissed on occasion, but he seemed more aggressive right now, more forceful.

She was suffocating in his embrace and tried to wriggle free. "What are you doing, Max?" she demanded. His body felt flushed and muscular against hers and while her body wanted to yield to him, her mind snapped into fight or flee mode and she kneed him without realizing she had hurt him.

Max immediately dropped to the floor with a hard thump as his knees collided with the hardwood floor. He moaned, "Awwww, Jesus, God Almighty, that fucking hurts so bad! Whaaaaaat?"

Sofia collapsed to the floor beside him and gently wrapped her arms around him immediately feeling bad for hurting him. She had no clue why it hurt so much or yet, what exactly she made contact with that could cause his virile young body to flop on the floor like she was a kung fu artist.

Max was still moaning and breathing hard, cupping his hands between his thighs.

"Oh, God, Sofia," he groaned, "that hurts so fucking much. I want you so badly. I want to touch you, Sofia. I can't stop thinking about you. I want to do more than just kiss you. Your lips, oh, jeez, I want you, Sofia. I swear to God, if I can't have you, I think I'm gonna die. I'm telling you, I can't go on like this. You're killing me!"

Catalina Ramos, Sofia's mother, suddenly appeared at the doorway. A short, stocky woman with graying hair and dark eyes like Sofia, her thick hands on her heavy hips, demanded, "What is going on in here my mi dulce niña? Eh, and you, big guy! Why are you still here with my niña? Shouldn't you be somewhere else?"

Max looked up at Sofia's mother and flushed, his cheeks hot and his eyes still tearing from the pain. He got up very slowly and shifted his clothes which had become disheveled.

"Uhhh, ummm, I am so sorry, Mrs. Ramos. I, uhhh, I…was just about to leave to go to my football practice, and I…"

"Then you better leave now before I have to call your mother and ask her why you keep coming around my house every morning. Don't you have something better to do than bother my Sofia? Huh?"

Sofia interrupted, "It's okay, Mama. Max was just trying to help me fill out this form so I could apply for the job. He has an uncle who works at the restaurant, right, Max? And he was going to take my papers to him later today."

Max played along and nodded his head up and down so hard he heard his neck snap and hoped Sofia's mother did not hear it, too.

"Yes, Mrs. Ramos, that is correct, ma'am. My uncle, see, he…uhhh, well, listen, Sofia, I really have to go now. Why don't you just email me your paper stuff and uhhh, I'll get it to my uncle later today.

"I guess I gotta go now. Bye, Sofia, and uhhh, Mrs. Ramos, yes, goodbye." And with that, Max grabbed his cell phone from the bed, picked up his shoes that he had thrown on the floor, and rushed out of Sofia's bedroom.

Sofia stared at the floor. She knew her mother was about to lecture her. She had been lecturing her ever since she got her period at twelve years old. *Do you know what boys can do to you now that you have your monthlies? Do you know, my carida? They only know one thing and it isn't to be your friend! They have those urges, niña, they have very strong urges and you have to be strong. Do you hear me?*

"Sofia," Catalina whispered to her daughter. "Awww, baby, can't you see? He loves you! Well, as much as a fifteen-year-old boy can love because honey, it ain't love right now. It's something else. And if you think I'm going to let that boy in your bedroom when I am not home, whoa, you will have to listen to your papa!"

Sofia sighed. She didn't want to hear this. She liked Max. She liked kissing him and when she talked with her girlfriends they giggled and laughed at her. And Jilly told me what Lucas had done to her in the dark corner of the hallway that caused her to get into so much trouble. And

Whitney, well, I think Whitney did that thing with a boy she met at summer camp last summer. She didn't tell me all the details, but I know, I know.

Sofia walked over and hugged her mom. "It's okay, Mama. I know what I am doing, and I promise you I will not end up like your cousin Besita. I do not want a baby. Mama, I'm only in high school. Please, I promise!"

Catalina hugged her daughter so tightly Sofia felt her breath whoosh out. "Oh, Carida, I only want the very best for you!! Catalina held her daughter's face in her hands and studied her face carefully, memorizing every inch of her. How could she ever confess to her only child that it was she and not Besita who got pregnant in high school and had her Sofia and moved in with her cousin to protect everyone's reputation?

The lies we tell, the stories we share, the ugly rumors we hide in the corners of our minds.

CHAPTER 5

Shaynee sat by herself in the computer lab at the library. It was a hot, blustery summer day but the library was always so cold Shaynee wore her sweatshirt. She looked around, her large eyes the color of smooth dark wet sand. "Jeez," she said to herself softly, "I must be the only dumb teenager here in the middle of summer. Everyone here is older than my mother. No, I take that back – my grandmother! I am such an idiot!"

At first, Shaynee thought to pack it up and leave when suddenly her screen made a strange noise. "Holy Mother of God!" Shaynee whispered gently to the computer screen. And there it was in full color! "It can't be! I can't be! I'll be goddamned if it is for real!"

The email was short and simple. Shaynee read it three times to make sure she wasn't misreading the words; they sounded too real to be true.

"Congratulations, Shaynee. You have a match with an 841cM DNA connection."

Shaynee read it again, slowly. What does cM stand for? I need to do more research she whispered to herself. But there it was. A match. Could this be just a relative? Or was it… Shaynee was afraid to think the words but she forced herself. She stared at the screen and murmured so no one else could hear her, "Are you my biological father? Are you for real? Who are you?"

Shaynee took out her cell phone and immediately texted her cousin. They were as thick as thieves with secrets, and she knew she could trust him.

Stetson – dude, you are not gonna believe what I am finding. Meet me at Starbucks tonight before dinner so we can chat. Can't text this shit – it's too much. DO NOT tell your mom 'cause she'll tell mine!!! Love, cuz

• • •

Berkley Roscoe was twenty years old and finishing her bachelor's degree. She and her identical twin, Brynley had gone their separate ways right after high school. Brynley went to New England Culinary Institute, NECI for short, in Vermont. She was passionate about her cooking and wanted to open her restaurant one day. She and Berkley were extremely close in everything from their love of old music, retro clothes, blue-eyed boyfriends, and most importantly – sharing secrets. Berkley loved to eat everything Brynley prepared for her, and

Brynley leaned on Berkley all through school for help in math and English. They were a perfect match.

While Brynley had finished her culinary degree and was busily chefing in some bougie high-end restaurant in the city, Berkley was finally concluding her teaching degree. She only had to complete her student teaching in the fall and then she could look for a full-time teaching job. And she didn't care where that was; in fact, the farther away from her parents the better. She needed to branch out. But this was summer, and she wanted to feel free and easy before her job search — before the real world closed in on her and she had to finally become that adult. Her mother warned her about being too frivolous, too carefree, too everything.

Regina Roscoe was so rigid, so pressed about rules and careers and the future for her daughters that Berkley felt squeezed to the point that she felt her throat constricting, her airwaves closing and her world collapsing.

"Mom!" she exploded, "You are not letting me enjoy my absolute last time not having to follow a time clock, report to a job, be attached to rules, have tons of restrictions. I mean, c'mon, lighten up a bit, please!"

Reggie closed her eyes, took off her glasses, and rubbed them gently. She loved her twin girls, and as identical as they were in physical looks, their personalities were as different as night and day. Brynley was mature, responsible, soft-spoken, and determined while Berkley was impulsive, reckless, loud, and filled with a charming magnetism that drew everyone to her.

"So," sighed Reggie audibly, "my darling daughter, what

exactly did you have in mind for the last summer of your life – as you have described it?"

Berkley smiled and Reggie could not help but smile back. Berkley had that magical touch, a powerful magnetic personality that made everyone in the room want to be on Berkley's team, in her group, and be a part of her cohort. Reggie knew her daughter had a special touch and it worried her. Sometimes late at night in bed, Reggie would quietly pray to God that Berkley would make the right decisions, be safe, and yes, even be cautious. She knew Berkley would be a phenomenal teacher one day because her students would absorb everything she would share with them, but, oh dear God, let her get there – and soon!

"Well, Mom," began Berkley, the twinkle in her hazel eyes bursting with joy, "there is this unbelievable softball camp up in the mountains and you know since I have been coaching this would be an incredible opportunity for my future as a physical education teacher and a coach if I could work as a counselor there for the summer. The pay isn't the best, I know, I know, but after this summer and after I student teach and then get my full-time teaching position, well, hells bells, Mom, I will be sitting pretty and can pay you back for the college bills and..."

"Baby girl, take a breath, please. I know this sounds good to you, but..."

"But what, Mom? You think Dad won't approve? He is never, ever around so what difference will it make?" Berkley was breathing hard, her high-arched brows raising in anger and her large, pouty lips spewing spittle uncontrollably.

Reggie was slowly losing her temper, and as usual, the upper hand with Berkley. Yes, her husband ran his own legal services firm and yes, he was rarely home as the office always needed his signature, his authorization, something he deemed significant. Reggie often wondered if he was having an affair with his secretary, but she pushed that way back in her mind, forcing herself to only think that Clemson Roscoe was a decent man, an honorable father, and husband, but sadly, a workaholic.

"Look, how about tonight I talk this over with your dad? Can you be patient and wait until then? I promise I will let you know first thing in the morning."

Berkley lowered her head. She knew she had won the fight even if it meant waiting it out till the next day. She closed her eyes, squeezed a small tear out of her left eye, and reached over and hugged her mom tightly.

"You're the best, Mom! I'm going to go upstairs and complete my application right now so I can get a jump on everything!"

And with that, Berkley flew up the stairs to her bedroom, laid down on her bed, and texted her twin.

Oh, wow, Bryn, you're not gonna believe it! I got Mom to agree to me going to this sick softball camp as a counselor. I mean, I already filed my application, and they already accepted me, but you know, I had to let Mom believe she gave me permission.

Softball camp was just how Berkley pictured it. She was able to work out with the girls, learn more coaching techniques from the camp leaders, and most importantly participate in the nightly team-building sessions in the gazebo.

The gazebo was huge. It was bigger than huge; it was ginormous. It was a structure that Berkley had never seen before. It was created out of pine wood with a huge Pagoda top. There were ten benches inside and the entire building sat on top of beautiful multicolored slate rocks.

In the evening the girls would sit on the benches or the floors and the head camp counselor, Maria Torres, would lead songs, tell funny stories, share some very scary *"dontstayinthewoodsalone"* stories, and the evening would conclude with each girl stating what they thought was special about that day.

The camp was going to be a long two weeks since it was

geared towards an elite softball program. On the second night, while we were sharing some funny stories, Maria told a story about her cousin, Ronnie. He was a goofy kid, she said and always managed to get in trouble no matter how hard he tried to be good. He and his family lived in Puerto Rico. One day Ronnie was playing baseball; he lived to play baseball and wanted nothing else to do in life but become a professional baseball player. Well, there he was one late afternoon playing in their sandlot as always. The neighborhood was poor, but everyone knew each other and looked out for each other. The kids built their own field using whatever materials they could scrounge up to use as bases.

It was Ronnie's turn at bat. Everyone in the outfield backed up because they knew how hard Ronnie could hit the ball. But Ronnie was not about to smack the ball on the first pitch. He loved the limelight, and he loved trying to psych the pitcher, so he was playing mind games with Teledo, his good friend. Sure enough, after hitting several foul tips the count was three balls and two strikes. The outfield held their breath. Teledo stared hard at Ronnie, the baseball turning round and round in his sweating hands behind his back. Teledo signaled no several times to his catcher before giving him the final nod. Teledo took a deep breath, pulled his arm in against his chest, released his wind up, and hurled the ball – dead center. Ronnie swung and smacked the ball so hard it flew high in the sky, passed the center fielder, and finally landed in the backyard of one of their neighbor's homes.

Ronnie, smiling and clapping his hands and whooping it up, ran the bases slowly. After all, no one was going to go after the ball. He stomped on first, then jogged to second jokingly sliding onto the bag, popped up, and walked/ran over to third. As he turned the corner at third, he somersaulted over the bag, jumped up, and walked to home plate.

It was the final home run of the game since it was the winning run so the players were shaking hands and laughing and high-fiving each other before Ronnie reached home. Once Ronnie tramped on home plate, dust flying up from the cracked plastic plate they used for home, he smiled at everyone and then ran out into center field.

His friends were screaming at him, yelling "Where ya going?" and "C'mon, man let's to the beach", but Ronnie did not look back. He was going to find his ball.

Ronnie jogged to the home-made rickety fence that separated the field and the neighbor's yard and then with one leap he easily scaled over the fence. There were bed sheets and towels and undergarments hanging on a long clothesline. Ronnie ducked under the flowered designed bed sheets and then came to a sudden halt.

Ronnie immediately homed in on his baseball resting innocuously in the grass, but his eyes opened wide as his head jerked suddenly beyond his ball to the most gorgeous woman Ronnie had ever seen! She was lying on her back in a lounge chair sipping a cold drink wearing very dark sunglasses, a large straw hat, and absolutely nothing else!

And what do you think Ronnie said when he saw this incredible woman?

Before Maria could share Ronnie's shocked comments, a deep male voice emanating from the gazebo steps boomed large and loud, "Well, dear cousin, I simply said, 'Excuse me, madam, but I have come to collect my baseball and I do apologize if I have interrupted your sunbathing activity!'"

The entire camp gasped at this stranger. Maria jumped up from the bench, ran over to him, and embraced him with a huge hug. She stepped back, faced the girls, and said, "Girls, it is my honor to introduce to you…my cousin, Ronnie!"

Ronnie grinned from ear to ear, his white teeth sparkling in the faded lights from the roof of the gazebo. He stood there in his baggy brown shorts, a wrinkled Nike tee shirt, and a dirty New York Mets baseball hat. He had the thickest black hair I have ever seen, a long straight nose, and the most magnificent light brown eyes.

CHAPTER 6

Cindy quickly finished her chores in the stables, mucking the stalls, rubbing down the horses, and spreading the fresh hay throughout each stall. She loved rubbing down her beasts as she lovingly called them and made sure she hugged each one around their large warm necks and placed a kiss on their wet noses.

In the corner of the stable was a small office filled with extra saddles, buckets, halters, leads, various medicines that she did not know what they were used for on the horses, and some extra blankets. But the most important part of the office was a large, soft, and comfortable deep blue chair made out of Naugahyde.

Cindy sighed slowly and deeply. She was exhausted from the day. She loved every minute of it. She was in charge of walking the horses with the campers. Each day her group of campers became more and more at ease with Cindy and the horses. Cindy loved getting to know her campers' names and she loved hearing them call her by her name although for many of them pronouncing her name was not an easy task.

Each camper was a special needs child brought to this camp for the sheer enjoyment of a summer experience. Cindy was not given the exact description of each child's disability, only that she knew she had to be patient, gentle, and loving. And she was. Whether she was fixing Anika's braids first thing in the morning or helping Coby hold onto the reins carefully or her favorite – she knew she wasn't supposed to have favorites – but Jasmine tore at her heartstrings. She would run to Cindy as soon as she saw her heading towards the ring and hug Cindy so tightly she would gasp and lose her breath. Jasmine always held Cindy's hand wherever they went and Cindy knew the girl would be a part of her heart forever.

The campers were all finishing their dinner that evening and then there was a special concert that night put on by a mom and a dad who sang and played their guitars. Cindy would eventually attend the show, but right now she collapsed in the chair. After letting her body give in to the heat and chores of the day, Cindy pulled out a letter that she had folded in her pocket earlier that day.

It was a letter from her best friend, Riley. Riley, who befriended her on her very first day at Wells High School and was always there for her, had written to her. She knew Cindy had a cell phone because the two girls texted all the time, so getting a letter was extra special and Cindy could not wait to relax and read it.

The envelope was neatly addressed to Cindy at her campsite. Riley was a stickler with her handwriting and Cindy yearned to print like Riley, but she could never quite get the way Riley printed her e's and a's. Riley's cursive was perfection, but her printing was like reading a Hallmark card.

Cindy held the envelope in her hand, stretching the moment of anticipation as long as she could. Even before she read the letter, Cindy knew she would read it over and over. She missed Riley. She missed her mom. Her mom was not doing well and hardly texted Cindy.

Cindy started crying to herself. "No, I'm not going to do that!" She shook her head and wiped her eyes. "I am the luckiest girl in the world to be at this camp and nothing is going to make me feel sorry for myself! Okay, Riley, let's go."

Cindy carefully and slowly slid her finger under the seal of the envelope. She wanted to preserve every minute of the letter. Opening the sticky label, Cindy gently pulled the folded paper out and held it in her hands. She unfolded the light blue stationary that was Riley's favorite and began to read, embracing the notion that Riley was right there in the stable room with her.

Dear Cindy...or Cindula as my mom likes to call you,

So, girlfriend, what's cooking? How are them horses doing for ya so far? Have any of those beauties kicked you off yet? Hahahah. Only kidding...sorta...

So let me catch you up on all our peeps. I'll save me for last, of course.

Hmmmm. Jilly...used to be close friends with her, but lately...not so much. Anyway, she is off somewhere in Europe with her parents. Don't even know when she'll come back... IDK...and who cares?

Lucas – well, I heard he and his stepdad are on some camping trip out west somewhere. He's not much of a communicator so I haven't even gotten any texts from that boy. Go figure...but I'm sure he's working out wherever he is cause he thinks he's gonna be the next football star for Wells...hahahah

Sondra, Junay, and Whitney – thick as thieves as usual. The three of them sucked up to Dr. Libertino and got some cushy job helping the new 9th graders coming in. They all think they are so cool and a bag of chips to go with it. They aren't getting any money, but I think they are adding up their hours for some service learning project or something like that.

Linette, I still call her that but she wants us all to call her Lane. That's cool for her. She is working at a camp her mother found so she can learn to speak her Filipino language – I think she called it Tag a long or maybe it's Tagalog...not sure...anyway, she texts me all the time and has been trying to teach me a few good curse words in her language. I'm not too good at it yet, but I'm trying.

The real juicy gossip is yep, you guessed it girl-friend – Sofia and Max. Well, it seems, and this is only hearsay ya know...well, it seems Max tried to go all.the.way. with Sofia and her mother walked in on her...holy shit...sorry...don't read that outloud to your little campers...so...Sofia has been grounded and Max is not welcome at their house right now... let's see what happens when school starts again.

Hmmmmmm...who else???? Piper and Tommy have been seen together at the mall and at the park but IDK if that means anything.

Oh...oh...oh...big...really big news... Shaynee was at the library when I happened to see her there. We talked for a few minutes, but she was pretty distracted. Said she was deep into ancestry and had found out some pretty important news about family stuff...not really sure what that means but she was pretty pumped about it and she swore she would get back to me when she knew more deets.

Okay...yes, ya know...time for me... I've been having a pretty awesome summer. My mom was able to send me to some camp for young chefs and I had a cool time. Got to learn some new recipes, but that's not the exciting part. Had to take some weird test to prove I knew where to put the raw chicken and the ground beef and the milk stuff. Anyway, it was a cake test and I passed it. You know that 'cake' means easy and not the devil's food kind! So cause I aced the test I got a job with a catering group.

It's really neat. I am the grunt cook in the team but that's okay. I love it. We travel all over the area setting up barbecues and shi...stuff. I saved some of the foods I made so I could let you taste them when you come home, which BTW is when???

And hey, Cindy...listen...my mom has been visiting your mom at the hospital. She wanted you to know that your mom has been too weak and tired to write to you, but she sends her love. I'll check with my mom and give you the skinny next time I write

Say hi to all those wonderful kiddies and I'm glad it's you and not me!!!! I'm never gonna be a teacher...ycchhhh.

Your friend,
Riley the wonder cook

Cindy finished reading the letter and placed it against her chest. She was worried about her mom, but she knew that if Dr. Maddox was checking in on her then that was a good thing. Or was it? She wasn't so sure. She knew her mom was still getting chemo for her triple-negative breast cancer, but her mom kept telling her that she was going to be okay after all of the treatments.

A tear slipped down Cindy's cheek and she quickly wiped it away. Suddenly, Cindy heard footsteps running in the stables.

"Cindy! Cindy! Where are you?" the young voice yelled out.

"I'm back here! Who's out there?"

"It's me, Cindy…it's Anika. Everyone is looking for you.

We are about to sing out good night songs and we need you. Cindy, please come out."

Cindy folded the letter carefully, slipped it back into the envelope, wiped her face again, and stepped out of the office.

Cindy smiled, even though it was a forced smile. "I'm here, Anika. I'm coming, sweetheart. Here, take my hand, and let's skip all the way to the big hall."

Together, hand in hand, Cindy and Anika skipping and singing headed out into the dusky evening.

CHAPTER 7

Little Emma stared at her Uncle Carl, her sapphire blue eyes sparkling in the soft lights in the living room.

"Unca Carl," she whispered softly, "when is my daddy coming here?"

Emma, just about to celebrate her 3rd birthday, was getting a little bit weepy and somewhat anxious about missing her father, Chip.

Carl stretched his legs and gently lifted Atticus's furry head off his lap. His colleague and close confidant from work, Neva, had asked Carl to dog sit while she was taking a two-week road trip to points unknown. Well, she sort of had an idea and she did text Carl whenever she landed in a motel for the night – just to check on Atticus – and Carl, of course, and especially Emma who Neva had come to love as well.

In addition to taking care of the loving and very large golden retriever, Carl was watching his niece, Emma. His brother Chip was finishing his last classes before beginning his student teaching. Carl was so proud of his brother for going after his dream. Chip had married Tarynda after she announced at a party for everyone to hear that she was pregnant. Chip, who had been working at Dick's Sporting Goods, decided he needed to follow his passion like his brother had and enrolled in Phoenix University. Working each day and concentrating on his studies each night until one night when Emma was just two, Tarynda came home and announced that she was tired of taking care of Emma and her boring job and she needed her freedom. Divorce papers followed shortly after, and Chip was able to procure full custody of his daughter. Tarynda wanted no part of being saddled, as she put it, with being a mother for the rest of her life. She had her own dreams and Chip, let alone Emma, was definitely not a part of her plan.

Carl and Chip's father, Harry, was helping Chip out until Harry was no longer capable of watching Emma. Following the death of their mother, Leila, Harry was inconsolable and found solace in the bottle. He lost track of time and sadly, lost track of watching Emma. Chip had come home one evening to find Emma sleeping on the kitchen floor, her thumb in her mouth and her diaper so soiled Chip found himself gagging as he gently picked her up. He gave her a warm bath, put on her favorite Elmo jammies, and fed her a late dinner.

Afterward, she fell asleep in his arms as he sang Carly Simon's "Mockingbird" which was Emma's favorite song. He laid Emma in her crib noticing that she was getting too big for the crib, making a mental note to talk to Chip about getting her a small girl's bed. Being a single dad was still so new to him and so many times he felt overwhelmed, exhausted, and worried sick that he was not doing a good job with Emma. Guilt, stress, and lack of sleep hung on him daily like an albatross, but when he held Emma in his arms and she giggled at his silly jokes and songs and hugged him tightly around his neck, his love for her was so deep that everything else that was overshadowing him slid away.

Chip woke his dad from his alcoholic stupor and escorted him to the guest room where his dad stayed most days. Chip knew he had to make other arrangements as his dad was no longer capable of safely watching Emma.

Carl and Chip, after a poignant reconciliation, bonded again. Carl, as Emma's uncle, took great pride in watching her whenever he could. Now that it was summer vacation, Carl wanted to give Chip that special time to focus on his studies.

Carl and Cassandra had been seeing each other regularly since he had returned to work. Carl was crazy about CC as he loved to call her. The two of them became so close spending hours with each other talking about a future together, sharing stories of their past and just holding each other.

Carl never knew how much of his life he had spent alone not realizing the tremendous gap that CC filled. She was his everything. He would call her in the morning to say hello if they were not at work, and then he would call her in the evening to see how her day was and to wish her pleasant dreams. Whenever they could be together, whether it was going for a walk, going to the movies, or even watching Cassandra shop for silly things at the mall, Carl felt complete when he was with her.

Cassandra loved helping Carl when he was taking care of Emma and this entire summer the three of them went everywhere. At times Carl could tell that strangers looked at them and smiled as though the three of them were a family on an outing. Carl smiled. He loved it all.

Carl was looking forward to a time when he could ask Cassandra to marry him. Being a part of Emma's life made Carl realize how strongly he wanted a wife, a family, and a continuation of the close relationship he was developing with his brother.

And now Atticus sat up, realizing that Carl was no longer his pillow. Carl closed the book he was reading to Emma and laid it on the coffee table.

"C'mere, my lovey," Carl said softly.

Emma, who was sitting on the other end of Atticus, slid off the couch, patted Atticus as she landed, and waddled over carefully to Carl. Carl scooped up his favorite niece and smothered her gently in his arms. She smelled of baby shampoo and lavender soap. He wiped a lonely piece of macaroni and cheese from her chubby cheeks and kissed her forehead.

"Oh, my little angel," he murmured. "Your daddy is coming over tonight because we are going to celebrate someone's very special day tomorrow! Do you know who that might be?" Carl had a twinkle in his eyes as he looked upon his niece. She was named Emma after his sister who sadly had committed suicide when she was only twenty years old.

Carl made a personal commitment to himself that he would never stop being in Emma's life and making sure she knew that between her father and her uncle, she was loved deeply. Staring into Emma's pudgy face, Carl smiled. There was a soft knock at the front door and Carl knew it was Cassandra. She was coming over to help celebrate Emma's birthday.

"C'mon in, CC," Carl said in an easy voice so as not to startle Atticus who was already up on his feet and plodding over to the front door, his padded feet making soft thumping sounds on the hardwood floors.

Cassandra opened the door gently and Carl swore she just floated in. Her smile lit up the room and her dark chocolate eyes matched her dark auburn hair. Cassandra pulled her hair back and laughed, "Oh, my that wind has blown me away today. I must look a mess!"

Carl shook his head, "Oh, CC, you are the brightest star in the sky. You could never, and I mean never look like a mess to me."

Emma giggled, "CC, you a mess today. You so messy. You so messy."

CC jogged over to the couch and snatched Emma up in her eyes. "Oh," she chuckled, "so you think CC is a mess to you?" And with that, Cassandra took her hand and playfully tickled Emma all the way up to her hair where she tossed those soft curls into a twirl.

Atticus wanted in on the play as he jumped up to CC and rubbed his wet nose on her arm.

"Oh my goodness," said Cassandra in a mocking tone, "did I forget to give you a quick rub behind your ears?" And with that, while still holding onto Emma, CC bent down and squeezed Atticus and rubbed him softly behind his ears. Atticus closed his eyes and licked CC on her leg until she squirmed and said, "Okay, we're good. We're good. How about we all sit down now?"

Cassandra plopped down next to Carl, letting Emma drop in her lap. Emma squeezed CC around her neck and planted several kisses on her cheek.

Cassandra beamed. "My…my…little Emma is so full of loving today – aren't you my sweetie?"

Emma giggled. Her mouth wide open and she leaned forward and delicately bumped her forehead into Cassandra's.

"CC," asked Emma, "Will you be my mommy?"

CHAPTER 8

Neva loved traveling. Ever since she was a teenager she had dreamed of backpacking across Europe, staying in hostels, speaking her broken French in France and her more competent Spanish in Spain.

Those dreams were just that – dreams. Getting married in college, losing the baby, divorcing the no-good sonofabitch loser husband, and then getting busy teaching. She loved teaching, but the ache in her heart to travel was always there.

One of her favorite things about teaching – besides the love of the job itself – was summer vacation. She had no desire to become an administrator. Who wanted to be an assistant principal and dole out discipline day in and day out? And then, more importantly, summers would become a thing of the past since those people worked year-round. Ycccch, thought Neva. Nope, I'm going to take advantage of my summertime and do what I want to do and if travel is a part of it, then by God I'm going to travel.

And so she did. Before adopting Atticus, Neva finally joined numerous tours that showcased France, Italy, Spain, and Amsterdam. Neva thought about purchasing one of those smaller RVs so she could bring Atticus with her during her local trips, but then she wanted to be totally unencumbered. And so she was able to see the Hoover Dam, Niagara Falls, and the Grand Canyon to list just a few.

This summer, however, Neva wanted to stay closer to home. She wanted to hike the Appalachian Trail starting in Maine. She wasn't sure how long she would be able to go, maybe as far as Virginia, but she wanted to try.

Neva had camped for several nights, but tonight she needed a real shower, a porcelain toilet, and a bona fide mattress to sleep on for hours if she so desired.

Dinner was delicious… The local diner served up home-cooked meatloaf, soft buttery mashed potatoes, mounds of local squash, and hot billowy buns. She was in heaven. She had been eating out of vacuumed packed dinners designed for hikers and while it satisfied her hunger it did little to satisfy her culinary delights. She laughed out loud to herself, "Wait till I share these foods with Alisa Saper." Alisa, the most popular foods teacher in the district, was one of her favorite colleagues at school. They had gone out to dinner a few times especially this past spring when Alisa had confided in her some of the horror stories she had learned about Beverly.

Beverly had been institutionalized and as far as Neva knew she was still there getting some very serious therapy. Well, she definitely needed it, thought Neva.

Dinner was done too soon, so Neva made her way back to the motel. It was a small family-run motel – The Bertha Berkshire and Sons. Neva didn't mind. It was clean and comfortable. Neva had been on the trail for over a week now and relaxing in a motel with all the technology made her realize how much she missed civilization. The trail was a wonderful trip, she nodded to herself, but she missed her cell phone, missed her cable televisions, missed her own bed, and especially Atticus.

It was getting very late and she was getting very sleepy with such a full stomach, but she made a mental note to call Carl in the morning to check on her lab. She knew he was babysitting his adorable niece, Emma as well as dog-sitting for her.

Neva couldn't stop yawning. Okay, okay. The bath eased all my old and aching bones and the local shampoo still smells luxurious, but I am going to crash in this extremely comfortable bed and sleep till noon.

Neva slipped on her favorite cotton pajamas from TJ Maxx and slid under the thick comforter. She picked up the remote and clicked on the television to TNT, Turner Network Television, and settled in to watch one of her favorite old Doris Day movies.

Neva was in a deep sleep. She was dreaming, her rapid eye movement flying back and forth. She was climbing up the mountain, but every few feet up, she kept sliding back down. Her hands reached up to grab hold of the rock, a tree root, anything, but her knuckles slid across the blackened rock, cracking open her dry skin so that the blood slowly oozed from her knuckles and the warm liquid sluiced down her wrist and swirled around her elbow. She wanted to cry, but this was not the time to feel sorry for herself. She needed to get to the top. Atticus was on top and he was whining. *Was he hurt, she thought? Why would he be crying? I need to reach him. I must get to him before…before…*

Neva felt herself slipping down the mountain again, her bruised body colliding into the sharp points of the shale. Her pants were torn and the small scratches widened into large gouges and blood flowed slowly down her leg pooling into her hiking boot.

She wanted to scream for help, but she knew no one was around. *I am such a fool to ever think I could go rock climbing on my own. Why did I even bring Atticus with me? I thought I left him with my friend. Oh, no! Maybe something has happened to Carl and that's why he dropped Atticus off. But at the top of the mountain? Didn't he see me?*

Neva could swear she heard her cell phone ringing. *It's Carl, she thought. He's calling me. He's letting me know why he had to drop Atticus off. And he'll come back for me. I know he will. I know he will. Oh, dear Jesus, I'm falling…I'm falling.*

THUD. Neva grabbed her head. She opened her eyes and realized she was on the floor. She must have hit her head because it was throbbing. She was tangled in the blankets and they must have twisted her so much she glided right off the bed.

And that was her cell phone. It was ringing. Who in the

hell is calling me in the middle of the night? Damn, it must be Carl. Where is my phone? Where the hell is my phone?

Neva sat up and reached for the nightstand. She stretched her arm and twisted the knob on the lamp and suddenly the room was flooded in a soft yellow glow. The cell phone, still ringing, was laying innocently next to the light.

Neva reached for it, pressed her finger on the speaker icon, and shouted, "Carl! Carl! Are you okay?"

But before she could say another word she heard a soft familiar voice.

"Neva? Neva? Is that you?"

Neva's eyes were still blurry from her dream sequence, and she tried to focus to see who had called her. She blinked several times, but there was no name on the cell, only a phone number. She did not recognize the phone number, but the voice…who was that?

"Neva," the voice continued softly at first, but gaining in volume little by little.

"Neva, it's me. It's Beverly."

Neva's mouth dropped open. Why would Beverly be calling me? And before she could even say how are you, Beverly, the screaming cry of a wounded bird pierced through Neva's eardrum like a poisoned arrow.

"GET ME THE FUCK OUT OF HERE! NOW! THEY ARE TRYING TO KILL ME! YOU GOT TO GET ME OUT OF HERE! THEY ARE POISONING ME WITH THEIR DRUGS! I NEED YOUR HELP! TELL THEM I'M OKAY! GOD DAMN YOU! LISTEN TO ME AND

GET ME OUT OF HERE BEFORE THEY KILL ME! THEY…"

The phone went dead. Neva, her eyes cleared and stunned, stared incredulously at the quiet phone resting in her hand. What the hell just happened? How did Beverly? Why did Beverly?

Neva touched the back button on her phone to see recent calls and realized the phone number that just called her must have been from the hospital that Beverly was in. She would call in the morning, but certainly not now.

Neva unraveled herself from the blanket and climbed back onto her bed and wrapped herself in the comforter. She was shaking. Her dream was bad enough, but to be woken out of her deep sleep to hear Beverly screaming at her shook her to the core. Sleep would not find Neva that night.

The cell phone was still clutched in Neva's hand. She had not put it down. She looked at it again. The time… oh, damn, what time was it in California?

Neva scrolled down in her favorites and pressed gently on her screen.

The cell phone was ringing. *Oh, pick up, pick up, Sis. C'mon.*

"Hello?"

"Kathleen? It's me, Neva. How ya doing, my favorite sister?"

Kathleen laughed. "Oh, sure, big Sis…I'm your only sister so you better love me best."

"Oh," Neva found her laugh, deep down. "Oh, boy, I do

love you, my girl. Say, I was wondering, well…you see, I still have a few days left of my summer vacation. Are you up for some special sister time?"

Kathleen did not hesitate to answer, "Boy, would I? How soon can you get across the country? I'm just finishing up a big article and I would love for you to read it before I send it in.

"And I don't mean putting all your little red marks everywhere!"

"Aw, c'mon, girlfriend, you know I only use purple!"

Kathleen chuckled. "Get yourself out here. I can't wait to hug you. I miss you so to the moon and back!"

"Kathleen," Neva started sobbing and couldn't stop. "If you only knew how much I miss you, too! I will be on the plane tomorrow. I'll call you when I'm at the airport with all of my details. Sweet dreams, sweetheart!"

"Right back at ya, Sis!" Kathleen sighed.

Neva found the large red circle to end her call, sighing softly as she pushed her finger into the X, placed her cell phone on the nightstand, and fell into a restless sleep immediately.

CHAPTER 9

"I don't want to go with you," whined Lucas to his step-father, Walter. "I have to go to football practice. I want to make the team and I am not going to get suspended this summer. I have not been in trouble and I don't plan on getting in trouble. Especially for missing practice."

Walter looked carefully into Lucas's soft blue eyes, the same gentle blue as his mother, Julie. But Lucas was not an agreeable even-tempered young man. He was an angry, belligerent, confrontational teenager. He had witnessed too much, been exposed to evil and his heart was cold, hardened by his biological father's perverse actions towards him.

It had been almost seven years since that night that Lucas ran away from when his father had molested him in bed, but the nightmares still plagued him. He saw his therapist, Miss Anna, on a regular schedule, and while she was kind and compassionate with him, her words were still not able to dissolve his anxieties and more importantly – his rage.

Walter Young had saved Lucas that horrific night when Lucas hid in the freezing cold night of the elementary school's playhouse. Following that night, a true and respectful relationship had developed between his mother and Walter which ultimately led to their marriage after Julie had divorced Angelo.

Walter was extremely understanding and patient with Lucas, but Lucas did not want another father, and Walter was African American, which was difficult for Lucas to deal with. It should not have been complicated, but for Lucas, it was a personal struggle and one that he would eventually have to accept – hopefully with the help of his therapist. But he wasn't there yet. And he was not sure who he was half the time questioning his experiences and the emotional damage he carried.

Lucas tried to convince himself that it wasn't Walter's race that caused the rift; it was any father figure. And yet it was Lucas who scrawled the racist epithets on the school wall. It was Lucas who cringed at the thought of being a part of an interracial family. Even though his principal, Dr. Libertino, shared her own interracial family background with him, Lucas was struggling.

The hardest part, Lucas recognized, was that Walter was a good guy. He was kind and loving to his mother. Angelo, Lucas recollected, was never nice to his mother. In fact, he was always rude and nasty. Lucas could never understand what his mother saw in him.

Lucas thought about the apology letter his father sent him. He had ripped it up and thrown it away. He wanted no part of his father, no matter how many times that man apologized.

"Lucas?" Walter was standing in his bedroom doorway, his thick shoulders brushing the sides of the door frame. Walter was being patient, but time was getting away from him. He was off duty this weekend and probably wouldn't have another weekend off for almost a month.

"You know, Lucas," Walter urged carefully, "I know there is football practice, but it is early in the season and I thought you and I, well…I thought…"

"I don't mean to disrespect you," Lucas interrupted, "but don't you think I need to be here? I mean, I messed up last summer…"

Walter did not want to go over this again. He took a deep breath and said a bit more aggressively, "Look, I checked with your coach. I told him I needed to spend time this weekend for some special time between us and that you would be afraid of losing your position and…"

Lucas glared at him. "You spoke to my coach? You actually went up to him and said that you needed some special daddy time? You are not my daddy and you never will be and I don't need you asking for favors from my coach! Do you hear me?"

"I'm not asking for favors. I'm not asking you to do anything but come with me this weekend. I'm not gonna beg you, young man, but I think you know me well enough by now to see that I want something else between you and me. I want an understanding. I know I cannot replace your father…well, I don't think you want that man in your life anyway I'm thinking, but I know that you and I, well, Lucas, damn, this is really hard on me, too.

"You know how much I love your mom. And every time she sees you getting upset she wants to fix it. She's a fixer. She loves you and she wants to make everything all right again. She knows she can't erase what happened, but give me a break here, son, and let me try and see what you and I can create…together. We are a family, Lucas…we just need to accept who we are and where we are going as a family. We need to move forward and stop living in the past."

Lucas wiped his nose and then wiped his snot-covered hands on his shorts. He hated getting so emotional. He needed to be a man but damn, this was never going to get easy for him, unless, shit, unless he sucked it up and let Walter feel that he tried his best.

Lucas bent over and picked up his weekend bag. "Well, shit, Walter, let's get the fuck outta here before I change my mind."

Walter smiled, placed his large bear-sized hand on Lucas's neck, and said, "Thanks, Lucas, but when you're around your mom, can you at least cool it on the curse words? You're making her cringe every time you use those words."

Lucas nodded and followed Walter to the car.

Walter let Lucas sync his Spotify music with the car radio. Walter was not too excited about Lucas's choice of music, but it was a small sacrifice and the ride was not going to be too long.

Lucas stared out the car window watching the terrain change from his small town filled with homes and town-homes and stores to the highway and finally to farms surrounded by rolling hills. He had to admit – it was beautiful. The sky was a brilliant blue with a few clouds floating by. He took a deep breath and felt his body relax. He was glad he changed his mind, but he wasn't ready to let Walter know that just yet. He couldn't ever remember going on a weekend trip and the new experience was exciting and a bit scary all at once.

Walter had bought him his own fishing rod and they were going to stay in one of Walter's buddy's cabins. A camping weekend filled with 'men talking crap, men eating junk food, men farting and telling dirty jokes' was exactly how Walter had framed it.

Lucas found himself being lulled to sleep as his eyes felt heavier and heavier as he stared at the ever-increasing mountain range, the farms dotted with cows and sheep, and hearing Walter hum along to some old music he had quietly switched over.

CHAPTER 10

Two months ago

Riley sat at the picnic table with Cindy, Lane, and Jilly. They were chatting and staring at their cell phones simultaneously. Every now and then one of them would stop and share something from TikTok or Snapchat from their phone.

"Jeez," whined Jilly, "Would ya look at this picture of Taylor Swift? What was she thinking dressed like that?"

"Ooooh," piped Cindy, "Can I see? Can I see? I love Taylor Swift. I would love to go to one of her concerts!"

"Uhhh," added Lane, "Aren't you always wearing one of her tees all the time? And you said you bought it at her concert. Duh…were you lying you silly bitch?"

Cindy's neck flushed crimson and it spread up through her face causing her to blink it had happened so quickly. Cindy's heart started racing and she knew the worst would be coming if she didn't control herself immediately.

She stared over at Riley who nodded slowly as though she were communicating silently. Cindy could hear Riley counting in her head with her – 1…2…3…breathe…1…2…3…breathe.

Cindy's chest was heaving and she closed her eyes.

Lane looked at Riley and said, "What! Did I say something wrong? C'mon! She's lying and you all know that!"

Riley gave Lane one of those 'shut up for now' looks and Lane stared right back.

Cindy opened her eyes, took one more slow, long breath, and said, "You know, Lane, you are right. I never went to one of her concerts because I didn't have the money. I bought that tee shirt at Walmart when they were having a sale.

"I guess I just wanted to fit in. You get that, huh?"

Lane shrugged and let her hand smooth out her short, cropped hair. Lane was being schooled in increasing her tolerance and considering she had asked her friends to accept her in her new role, well, who was she to judge?

"Yeah. Cindy, hey, I'm sorry. It's cool. Hell, I bought a poster at Target and you know what I did?"

The girls stared at Lane and in unison said, "WHAT!"

Lane looked at Cindy, then Riley, and finally at Jilly. She shrugged her shoulders, looked up at the sky, and blew out her breath. "I put that poster on my wall and then I took a sharpie and signed it as though it was personally autographed! And I never told anyone that I did it!

"So, yeah, Cindy. I frigging get it. You're cool and I'm sorry for being a douchebag sometimes."

Cindy smiled, her breathing relaxed and her heart had calmed down. She looked at Lane and whispered, "Shit, it's all good. That's why we all hang together. Cause I can say anything and I won't be made fun of. Well, at least not by any of you. And, well I'm okay with anything you all say, too!"

Riley laughed and looked up at the next table in front of them. It was Shaynee and her cousin, Stetson. Those two were inseparable. Riley didn't realize it but she found herself staring at the two of them, their shoulders almost touching they were so close.

The two of them were wearing tee shirts and Riley was focusing in on Shaynee's left elbow. She had never noticed it before but there was a heart-shaped mole right above her elbow. Not that something like that was earth-shattering or worthy of late news, but Riley was casually letting her eyes roam over to Stetson, and damn! Stetson had the exact heart-shaped mole above his right elbow. What the hell?

Is that even physically possible? She knew they were cousins and cousins shared a lot of genetics. Growing up in a household with two doctors for parents, Riley picked up a ton of information she stored in her brain under 'useless shit' and very rarely remembered any of it.

But identical moles? Hmmmmmm. It just got her thinking. She was so deep in her thoughts she did not hear the other girls until finally, Jilly poked her in the ribs.

"Hey, Riley…come back to earth…girl where did you go?"

Riley turned her head and realized that the girls had been asking her questions and she had no clue what they were talking about.

"Uhhh. Hey, I'm sorry. Listen, you guys, I gotta go talk to Shaynee for a bit. Catch up with you later." Riley scooped up her backpack, slung it over her shoulder, and left the table.

She walked over to where Shaynee and Stetson were sitting. Riley sat down across from them and smiled. She bent over and retied her purple Chuck Taylors. She had just purchased them right off of Amazon and she was very proud of her purchase. But truth be told, she just needed time to think, and pretending to tie and retie her shoes gave her those few extra seconds for her brainwaves to go back and forth like a pinball machine.

Riley sat up and looked at Shaynee and Stetson who were eyeing her, both of them with their eyebrows scrunched up into their forehead. Ahhhhh thought Riley, here is another example that screamed from another universe deep in her head. Her investigative curiosity was tickling at warped speed and she was having very deep personal conversations with herself telling her logical brain that this went beyond cousin coincidence.

Riley cleared her throat and began, "Well hey, you two cuzzies. How's it hanging? Like what's going on in your life that is so interesting that you didn't even sit with us today? Huh? Do we have cooties or something?"

Shaynee looked puzzled. She stared at Riley and squinted

her light brown eyes. "What do you mean, Riley? Stets and I were shooting the shit and planning what we were going to do this weekend."

Riley gave a half smile. She looked over at the girls hoping they were not interested in whatever Riley was doing with Shaynee and Stetson. Fortunately, they were busy giggling over something that Riley figured was stupid and immature.

She continued, "Well, it looked to me like you two were plotting a murder of some kind the way you were sitting and conspiring." Riley forced a laugh. She was hoping to get some kind of rise out of one of them, preferably Stetson, who always looked like he was confused about something. He had that *Idontknowwhatsgoingoninlife* look most of the time, but his dazzling smile always had the girls ooohing and ahhhing over him. I guess they like the guys cute and dumb, acknowledged Riley, to herself. Okay, she chided herself. Move on, girl.

Stetson, even with his innocent and naïve look, liked Riley and he loved teasing her. She was cute and smart, and at times a bit too standoffish and intellectual for him, so he liked to bust her chops. Stetson laughed, "C'mon Really-Riley. Who do you take us for? I mean just because we have our own little secret club doesn't mean you get to drop in here and pick us apart like we are the enemy. Duh, do you think we are plotting something, huh?"

Riley smiled. She loved it when Stetson teased her. She did not have any siblings and it took her a few years to understand that Stetson was only trying to provoke her.

He was always playing with her name calling her Really Riley or Rockin' Riley or Ridiculous Riley.

Shaynee and Stetson both started laughing and for some unknown reason, a light bulb exploded inside Riley. She saw the way both of their lips curled up on the side when they laughed and that one eye tooth on both of them was identical and frigging sharp!

And then their eyes! That striking light brown – what color would you say it was? Amber, that's it. And their eyebrows. Holy moly – the way their eyebrows arched up making their noses look even longer.

Riley shook her head. Damn, she said to herself. I feel like I'm looking in a mirror when I see them side by side. I guess I never placed them right next to each other like this.

"Uhh, Shaynee," Riley began. "Oh, and Stetson, I am so sorry I burst into you two so rudely, but I gotta ask you… well, actually, Shaynee I gotta ask you first.

"Remember a few months ago you said you completed that Ancestry thing – you know the thing you spit into a tube and sent away?"

"Yeah, Riley, what of it?" Shaynee was a bit put off because this was a very private thing she did. She did not even tell Stetson about it because she was scared for him to know what she was doing. She didn't think Riley would bring that up, especially in front of anyone else.

Riley saw how uncomfortable she had just made Shaynee and instantly felt sorry to have broached the secret. But Riley was stubbornly determined. She was on a roll and did not want to stop right there.

"Oh, Shaynee, I'm sorry, girl." She looked at Stetson and lowered her eyes. "Hey, Stetson, I have to apologize because Shaynee had confided in me and I think I just broke that confidence. I am so sorry, but, Shaynee, listen…"

Shaynee stood up suddenly and grabbed her books. Her eyes went to a dark coffee color and her cheeks were flushed. "I trusted you, Riley Maddox. And I am totally certain that I will never…ever…believe in you ever again!"

And with that, she turned and was just about to leave when out of nowhere Barbara Atkinson suddenly appeared at their table. Shaynee almost bumped right into Ms. Atkinson causing her books to slip out of her hands, float down, and create a halo of bound materials around her.

Ms. Atkinson coughed as if that action could control the sudden chaos of the three teenagers. Each one's face had a different look from anger to sorrow to total confusion. Ms. Atkinson quickly absorbed all three expressions analyzing a possible inflammatory scene that was about to combust. "Well, hello there…and may I ask if everything is alright in your world today?"

Riley stared at her administrator. Ms. Atkinson was not her favorite because she was always sarcastic and nasty. No one in her group liked Ms. Atkinson and no one wanted to tell her anything important because they did not trust what she would do with the information.

"We are all just fine and dandy," said Riley in as snarky a tone as she could muster without getting called out for her insolence.

"Hmmmm," replied Ms. Atkinson, "it sure didn't look

like you were all having such a 'fine and dandy' time from my point of view." Barbara could smell a potential conflict from down the hall and around the corner, and she stared long and hard at Shaynee first, then Riley, and finally Stetson. Slowly, methodically, her gaze burned the guilt right to the top of their heads exposing any lies they may have been trying to hide.

Shaynee fidgeted. Her mouth was as dry as cotton candy and her fingers felt cold. She sensed other students staring at her. She hated being called out, especially by an administrator. She rarely got into trouble and right now she could feel the eyes of everyone around her. They were curious, their laser focus questioning the unfolding drama, and definitely excited to see the action. She despised being in the middle of anything uncomfortable. She did not want to lie and she did not want to share the conversation that she and Riley were having. It was none of Ms. Atkinson's business. It was no one's business except hers and Stetson's. And she had not been given the opportunity to clue Stetson in – yet. Riley had interrupted them and completely threw her off the entire conversation she had practiced in her head. She had wanted this to be perfect, loving, and somewhat shocking, and it was her story to tell and Riley had ruined it. All the time Shaynee had put in doing her private investigative work and her special moment was tarnished. Damn, she was angry and frustrated and wanted to scream as loud as she could, but this was not the place. She would deal with this later when she was alone with Riley and let her know what she had done.

She was tired of the way her lunch time had turned ugly and argumentative and she wanted to be finished with the conversation. "I'm fine, Ms. Atkinson and if you don't mind, well, I'm outta here. Shaynee bent down, picked up the books that were sprawled around her, got up quickly, turned, and walked away leaving Riley and Stetson with their eyes wide open and their arms whipping up in the air as though they were signaling to everyone near them that the party was over and to stop staring.

Ms. Atkinson homed in on Riley, her beady brown eyes burning a hole in Riley's forehead. "Are you sure there is nothing I need to know about? Because, young lady, if something happens here at Wells and I am not informed, well, I don't need to tell you what sort of consequences you will be facing."

Riley hated being threatened. She was a strong girl, confident but not cocky, and she was not one to back down from a standoff.

Riley took a slow breath, puffed out her chest just a bit, looked straight at Ms. Atkinson, and said as slowly as she could, "There is nothing you need to know, Ms. Atkinson, and quite honestly, if there was something significant to know here at Wells, you would be the absolute last person I would share that with – if you want to know the truth."

Riley spun around, slipped her arm through Stetson's, and waltzed him out of the dining area. Riley knew that what she had just said was rude and nasty and she was sure she was going to get into a heap of trouble for it. But she didn't care, and she didn't want to wait around to see Ms. Atkinson's reaction.

Barbara Atkinson stood there, her large hands resting on her hips. Her breathing was fast and erratic. Lately, every time she had an incident with a student she could feel her heart racing and her fingers tingling and turning cold. She hated that feeling; hated knowing she was not getting through to these teenagers. Was she losing her grip on how she disciplined? Being inadequate in her role as the main disciplinarian of the building was not the path she had intended. She wanted something more, something higher – she wanted her own building where students listened to her, feared her, and respected her. And so she stood there until the students around her stopped staring, bored with the lack of drama until she felt confident enough to walk away.

Stetson was nonplussed as he allowed Riley to guide him through the cafeteria and into the main hallway. They were turning the corner by the main office when Stetson stopped, pulled himself away from Riley, and said angrily, "What the hell got into you? I mean what just happened? Shayz and me were having a great time enjoying our lunch and then wham, bam, you come outta nowhere and spoil our day like no other."

Riley would not look at Stetson until they were far away from everybody, especially Ms. Atkinson, who she had left standing in the middle of all the picnic tables, her large hands on her hips and her mouth wide open in astonishment.

The bell was about to ring and students were busy opening and shutting lockers, swinging backpacks over their shoulders, and racing off to their next class.

Stetson pushed Riley into the purple-colored lockers and got right up into her face, his breath fast and hard. He was so close Riley could see the small hairs on his chin that were starting to sprout. Stetson would not be denied. He needed to know why Riley was doing this to him, to Shaynee. "Now, what is going on here?" Stetson whispered hard with spittle trickling over his lips and his voice rising to such a high pitch that Riley's neck prickled from his anger.

Riley fixated on Stetson's clear copper-colored eyes for a moment before she said a word. She took a slow, deep breath. She laid her arms on Stetson's shoulders and very calmly whispered to him so only he could hear her, "Stetson, my friend, I don't think you and Shaynee are just cousins. My friend, I think you and Shaynee are twins!"

CHAPTER 11

Riley loved summer vacation. She lived for the outdoors and would have slept outside by the large maple tree every night if only her parents had let her. Sometimes she would sneak outside with her sleeping bag, a cup filled with cookies and popcorn, and her cell phone. She would find one of her favorite movies on an app, curl up inside her sleeping bag, munch on her goodies, and sigh with total enjoyment.

Riley always sighed when she was in her nirvana. She didn't realize she was doing that until one night when Cindy was sleeping over before summer break Cindy had to tell her.

"Uhh, Riley, did you know that you groan really loud? I mean like a lot? You know you make these weird sounds. And last night you were so noisy that I heard you down the hall in my room. What were you dreaming that caused you to make those noises? Were you having a date? Were you cooking for a wedding or something?"

Cindy giggled knowing how silly she sounded. She sat up on the small couch across the room from Riley. Her bedroom was so spacious that Riley had a small couch, a desk, a queen-sized bed, a huge-ass dresser – Riley's words – plus a television mounted on the wall and a special desk just for her computer.

Cindy had the guest room down the hall which was even bigger than her own bedroom in her house. The guest room had a queen bed, a dresser, and a large desk plus a television. Sometimes Cindy asked Riley to stay over just because the guest bedroom seemed to relax her nerves. There was something special about the room that made Cindy feel calm; Riley named it, she said it was called feng shui, whatever that was, but…whatever…the room comforted her.

Riley laughed. "Damn, Cindy. I didn't realize you could hear me. I guess when I'm reading something I enjoy, or watching a movie and I, hell, I don't know, I think I moan out loud when I am in a complete state of happiness. Like when I cook something new and it turns out," Riley smacked her lips together, "Mmmmm, absolutely perfect!"

Riley looked at Cindy's confused face. Cindy's nose was scrunched up and her eyes behind her glasses were squinting. Riley reflected, "Is that such a thing, Cin? I mean don't you ever just sit back and feel totally content about your life or a movie or a book? Anything?"

Cindy looked down at the floor, her eyes staring at nothing. "I don't know that I am ever that happy. I mean, I'm not sad, you know…I…well…I just deal with my life as it happens. And when it doesn't happen well, like most of the time…I get anxious. So, no, Riley, I don't think I have ever felt the way you feel. Completely content, I mean."

Summer vacation, finally. And on that first day of no school, no homework, and no stress from parents about chores, Riley woke up, stretched, and eased her way out of her bed. She opened her curtains and let the full sun wash over her as though she were being baptized by the rays of the summer shine. A calmness spread over her and Riley took a deep, cleansing breath.

"This is definitely going to be a summer to remember," she said to her favorite old brown teddy bear who lay limp on her large blue bean bag in the corner. "No…no…no… you don't have to remind me to brush my teeth. I'll do it. Just let me enjoy this moment, would you?"

The soft fur on the teddy bear seemed to move ever so slightly and Riley took that as the answer she was looking for even though the breeze from her open window was probably the logical and scientific explanation.

Riley made her bed; she never forgot to make her bed because it was too important to come home and see all her stuffed animals relaxing on her pillows – a personal invitation that told her to curl up beside them and share her anecdotes about her day.

There was a pile of clothes on her dresser. It was her new uniform for the summer. Riley was supposed to go away to some culinary camp, but although she would have enjoyed going, Ms. Saper had offered her a unique opportunity for the summer – a real paying job!

Alisa Saper, her favorite teacher who taught all the food classes at Wells, worked for a catering company during the summer. Alisa was good friends with the owner of the catering company, Bobbie. The two of them had met in college while they were both picking up extra money working at the college student union kitchen. Alisa was majoring in what they called home economics while Bobbie was studying anything she found interesting. From art history to law and world geography, Bobbie loved learning. But more than anything, Bobbie loved cooking.

Alisa urged Bobbie to join her and become a teacher, but Bobbie wanted nothing to do with kids. "I hate kids," she joked. But Alisa knew she wasn't joking. Bobbie was the oldest of seven in her family and when her mother died when Bobbie was only fourteen, she had for all intense purposes become the surrogate mom of the group. So bottom line, she didn't want to have children of her own – she already lived that life.

But Bobbie Crandon's cooking was her passion and her escape. Even though going to college was more of an excuse not to be home so much, Bobbie knew there was a limit to how long she could manage to stay away from her family responsibilities. So, she took as many classes as she could, ran home afterward and cooked and cooked, and dreamed of a future where she was always in a kitchen.

By the time Alisa was in her first year of teaching at Wells High School, Bobbie had quit college, taken out a loan, and started her own barbecue business. It took off like a lightning bolt and Alisa was by her side every summer since then.

So when Alisa asked Riley to stay after class that day in May, Riley was completely stunned when Alisa asked, "Hey, Riley, what kind of summer plans do you have, girl?"

Riley shrugged, "Uhhh, my parents are sending me to some big-time culinary camp. It's a sleep-away cause it makes their life easier and I get to learn some more cool shi…stuff about foods." Riley laughed, "Maybe when I come back, I can even teach you a few things, huh?"

Alisa chuckled. "I'm sure you will! Just because I teach all about foods doesn't mean there aren't some things out there I still need to learn!

"But," Alisa continued a little hesitantly, "well, I was wondering…and you don't have to answer me right away… and you don't have to feel pressured just because I'm the one asking you…and you would definitely have to ask your parents…and…"

Riley burst in. "So, what!!! What are you trying to ask me" I'm gonna bust if you don't spit it out! Excuse me… that didn't sound very nice. I mean, Ms. Saper, you're filling me up with anticipation here. Just say it, please!"

"Okay," laughed Alisa. "I'll come right out and ask you. Instead of going to a camp, a cooking camp for goodness sake, how about you come work with me this summer at a barbecue catering company and learn firsthand how to make a thousand people happy all at once?"

Riley's mouth dropped open, and her eyes seemed to

bug out. "Are you for real? Do you really mean it? I mean… like that is so totally cool… I mean…really…you would want me to work for you?"

"Yes, Riley. That is if your parents agree with this new idea. After all, they probably have paid for your camp's tuition already and I don't want them to lose that money."

"Oh, pulllease, they don't care about the money. But that is so off-the-wall cool… I can't wait to go home and tell – not ask – my parents about this. I gotta go…like now…oh, and thanks, Ms. Saper. You are the bomb!!"

Riley was smiling as she slipped on her brown cargo shorts that she was told she had to wear along with a blue tee that read BOBBIE'S BBQ on the back in large black letters. Riley slipped on her headband as her auburn hair was still too short to pull back in a ponytail.

Her parents, Jeanine and Gunther, were a bit hesitant about her working at such an early age, but Riley strongly convinced them that being totally immersed in a cooking environment like a catering company would beat out a summer camp cooking experience that was just for fun. Especially, argued Riley, when most of the campers wouldn't know a thing about cooking other than going to a drive-through for their food.

"Come now, Riley," begged Gunther repeatedly, "your mother and I have placed you in the most prestigious cooking camp on this side of the country. Local chefs will be there. And, more importantly, you will be taught individually by Michelin chefs from all over the world and you want to give this up for some rinky-dink low-level barbeque company that hires high school dropouts?"

Jeanine interrupted, "Gunther, please. If this is something that Riley will enjoy for the summer instead of sending her away like we always do, then let her make that decision. She is getting to be a young adult, and I strongly believe…"

Now it was her father who interfered, "No, Jeanine, I will not allow it. Riley is much too young to be working for some disreputable company that we would never allow ourselves to partake in their fare and I am standing firm on this!"

Riley was losing her patience. Her parents rarely objected to anything she was interested in, so she was confused, angry, and annoyed.

Riley took a deep breath, stuck her hands on her hips and faced both parents, and said emphatically, "Look, you are both doctors. You are hardly ever here. I get myself to school. I make myself breakfast, and lunch and then I even make dinner for the both of you even though you never make it home on time to sit down with me.

"I am alone most of the time. I love you both. I know how hard you work. But, this is my summer. My time. And my teacher, my favorite teacher mind you, personally asked me if I was interested in the job. She trusts me. She believes in me. And I think it's about time that the two of you trust me to make this decision. Believe in me for knowing this is a good choice. I don't ask much of either of you. I never do. And now, I'm asking you to support me." Riley exhaled, her cheeks were flushed, and her amber eyes were misting over but she refused to cry. She clenched her hands together digging her nails into her palms and squeezing her lips tightly.

Jeanine smiled. Gunther looked down at their Persian rug and shrugged.

"Well, Gunther," said Jeanine. "I think it's high time we listened, really listened to our daughter. We need to be there for her, allowing her to make some choices, and should this one not work out for the better, well, then we need to be there to support her. Don't we, Gunther?" Jeanine pulled at Gunther's arms and at the same time pulled Riley into her.

"Hey, it's time for a group hug. Yes? C'mon now. Gunther, buck it up, mister. Your daughter is growing up in front of our eyes and we need to see the world through hers. Get in here, now!"

The three of them stood in their living room huddled together in a group hug, not realizing that it would be the last time the three of them would stand together surrounded by their love.

CHAPTER 12

everly knew the drill. She hated the drill, but she knew it forwards and backward. If she wanted out of this place, this mentally backward institution, then she had better show them – the bastards – that she was 'cured.' It wasn't going to be hard to do, but it was going to take some fortitude because it was all going to be fake. She was good at lying; she lied about Carl, and she lied about the teacher in the school before she was transferred to Wells, whatever that woman's name was. In Beverly's mind, that woman was a bitch and did not deserve to be remembered by name.

Beverly entered Dr. Ethan Carter's outer office very slowly, methodically, calculating her every move. The room was filled with cheap hanging copies of various Monet paintings. Beverly's favorite was the Weeping Willow and the one titled Sunflowers. There were several different versions of the Water Lilies and Beverly sneered at them. She did not want to bring any attention to the fact that she was impressed with anything in the office. She did not want to encourage small talk, any kind of talk with that snotty little secretary, Lillian.

The paintings were meant to bring warmth and a sense of peace, along with some positive spirituality. It made Beverly want to puke. But she had vomited once before on Dr. Carter's expensive carpet, and she thought that a repeat of that vile action was not going to win her any special compensation. She thought better of it and almost tip-toed over to greet Lillian, Dr. Carter's ancient secretary.

Lillian O'Neal, a petite elderly woman with a Dorothy Hamill haircut that had grown in all white years ago, was busy working on her computer. Her mascara was smudged from rubbing her dark brown eyes too often. Lillian needed to wear glasses, but she was too self-conscious about her looks to wear those clunky cheap pair she bought online so they lay quietly next to the computer.

She did not hear Beverly approach her and was stunned when a fist slammed down on her desk next to her computer. Lillian jumped from her seat; her heart pounding so hard she grabbed her chest automatically as if she could stop the throbbing. Her chair had fallen over when she had leaped up and now she stood still staring at Beverly with questioning eyes.

Beverly smiled and said with syrup dripping in her voice, "Oh, my, Miss Lillian. Did I startle you just now? Why, I am so very sorry. I did not mean to do that. I was reaching for your glasses, and, well, I guess I tripped over the carpet right here and had to catch myself from falling. Here, let me get your chair back in place for you." Beverly glided past Lillian's desk gently scooped up her chair and gingerly placed it behind Lillian.

Lillian stared into Beverly's beady eyes which were trying to grow as wide as her lies. Lillian was always ready with a smile and a welcome to all of Dr. Carter's patients, but this one…this one was the devil in disguise. Lillian never liked to discriminate or worse – stereotype any of Dr. Carter's patients, but she was troubled whenever Beverly entered the office.

Lillian could not quite put her finger on what was so disquieting about this patient, but there was something underneath, something dark and perhaps wicked that made her skin crawl.

Lilian took a deep breath, and picked up her glasses slowly, methodically, and too painstakingly unhurried for Beverly who started to tap angrily on the desk. Lillian knew this would irritate Beverly and smiled to herself.

"Good afternoon, Ms. Winewrought," Lillian declared carefully. "And how can I help you today?"

Beverly shuffled her feet and ran her fingers through her longer-than-usual hair. She was annoyed at having to wait and her attitude was nasty and the syrup in her voice turned bitter and thick. "You can get me in to see the doctor. I mean now. I don't have time to wait for another appointment, whenever the hell that might be. I need to see Dr. Carter and I mean today. This could be considered a damn emergency if you get my drift."

"Now, Ms. Winewrought, you know I do not approve of

your tone or your vulgarity in this office. And besides, Dr. Carter is with another patient at the moment. You said this is an emergency? Would you like to have a seat and wait awhile, or shall we arrange for his earliest appointment? Which would you like, my dear?"

Beverly despised Lillian's answer. Lillian acted so sweetly and motherly that Beverly wanted to snap her petite neck right in half. She automatically clenched her fists by her side. Her jaw clamped shut and her nose started twitching up and down. But Beverly knew better. This was not going to solve anything if she acted rashly and threw a fit. So she paused. She unclenched her fists and relaxed her mouth. And then she smiled. Beverly bent over and picked up a pen that she had knocked off the desk when she had pounded on it and gently placed it next to Lillian's computer.

"You know, Miss Lillian. I would greatly appreciate it if you wouldn't mind me sitting here in your lovely office while I waited for the good doctor. I mean, after all, I really don't have anywhere else to be right now since you have completely obliterated all of my outside activities."

Lillian held back a guffaw. Beverly was so manipulative, and Lillian knew it, but she had to play this game with her. Lillian had worked for Dr. Carter for over twenty years, and she knew a charlatan when she saw one. Lillian was not afraid of Beverly, but she also knew that Beverly was shrewd and calculating so whatever Lillian said next had to be carefully stated.

"Ms. Winewrought, you are certainly welcome to have a seat and wait for Dr. Carter. He is seeing his last patient of the day so I am sure he will be able to spend a few moments with you shortly. I do need to inform you that Dr. Carter does have a meeting to attend later today so I am not sure how long he will be able to meet with you this afternoon. Will that suffice, my dear?"

Lillian smiled at Beverly, showing all her newly dentured teeth. With her hands clasped together and her glasses falling over her nose, she patiently awaited Beverly's response.

Beverly knew she was backed into a corner. Lillian was giving her an opportunity to see the doctor but on his dime. Take it or leave it.

"Miss Lillian, you are just too kind." Beverly glared into Lillian's eyes with such malice that caused Lillian to stifle a small shudder. Beverly turned around and sat down in the large, overstuffed lounge chair near the door just in case she decided to leave.

Lillian sighed, took off her glasses, and returned to pecking at her keyboard even though she wasn't looking at what she was typing, she just wanted to appear busy for now.

CHAPTER 13

Benjamin was turning sixteen and Lila was concerned. The school year had finally concluded for the summer but that only meant that Lila would be busier than ever just on a different level. She was bombarded with principal meetings at the board, and if that wasn't bad enough, she was told that she was nominated to be chair of the Principals' Summer Retreat Committee.

"I knew I was going to be stuck with a committee," she told her assistant principal Barbara Atkinson. "As soon as I missed that important spring meeting, I had to reconcile with the fact that being so-called nominated for a chair position only meant that was how you were reprimanded for missing a meeting."

Barbara laughed mischievously. She understood only too well how much Lila hated being pulled away from school regardless of the reason. Managing the school, moving it forward academically, and developing a culture of professionalism and camaraderie among her staff would have been more than enough. But Lila wanted more and that meant ensuring her students were positively involved in as many aspects of high school life as possible from academics to sports to arts and drama and student government and everything in between.

Lila squinted at Barbara. "Don't make fun of me, missy," chastised Lila. "You are only a New York minute away from heading up the teacher interviews to fill in all of the vacant positions. Especially the one Beverly will not be returning to in the fall."

"Oh, really," questioned Barbara. "I thought that her position would not be vacated should she complete her medical program."

"She will not have to resign from teaching," Lila continued, "But she will no longer be teaching at Wells. That was a condition I demanded from our superintendent, which along with my missing a monthly principals' meeting only added to the *guesswhoisnominatedtoheadthesummerretreat!*"

Barbara knew when to back off her teasing. "On a positive note, Amelia, your top-notch secretary is the queen of organizing retreats. She has a notebook filled with ideas and agendas including a list of who can cater and who can provide freebie gifts for your illustrious group!"

Lila smiled. She wholly saw what Barbara was doing by shifting the conversation. "Thanks. I know I can always count on Amelia. And I know I can count on you to fill in for me when I am at that damn retreat. Bonding. Not what I envisioned for my summer goal. But, I will do what's necessary."

Lila closed her eyes and pretended she was in a deep-think mode. Barbara knew better than to interrupt or else be subject to more subbing for her principal so she stared out the window waiting and praying Lila wasn't coming up with more tasks for her to do.

Just at that moment, Amelie Goddard knocked softly at the door. "Excuse me, Dr. L., but your husband is on the line, and he says it's urgent. Shall I take a message, or do you want to speak with him now?"

Lila snapped her head up, opened her eyes, and answered, "Thanks, Amelia. I will go ahead and take it. Barbara, do you mind sharing my new summer task with Amelia? I'm sure as soon as you explain to her what I have to accomplish she will be on that like a bear on a honeycomb!

Amelia's large emerald eyes glowed with the admiration she had for Lila. She knew that when Lila gave her an assignment, she was allowed as much free rein as necessary and Amelia loved that challenge. She turned and left the room with great anticipation as Lila and Barbara heard her whisper to herself, "Yesssss!"

Barbara took this cue for her to leave as well and she said with much satisfaction, "Okay, let me organize my interview list and get going on that before all the best teachers are scooped up!"

Lila was left alone in her office and gazed at the phone for just a moment. Why was Darrius calling with an urgent message? They were supposed to be taking Benjamin out to dinner to celebrate his birthday. Was something wrong? She reached for the phone.

"Hi, baby," she said softly. "What's up, my love?"

"Lilly," he whispered. Lila knew he only called her that when he was worried.

"Talk to me, Darry," she responded.

"Baby, it's Benjy. Come home now, please. We need to deal with something and I don't want to talk about it on the phone."

"On the way right now." Lila hung up the phone, closed her computer, and grabbed her leather briefcase and bag. She was on the way out of her office when Gloria Lomack, the head of the counseling department, and Jeff Stineman, the Assistant Principal, bumped into her as they were heading into her room.

"Oooffff," muttered Lila. Seeing her two colleagues, Lila stopped, her hands still gripping her bag and her briefcase that she almost dropped after rushing right into the two of them outside her door.

Jeff opened with, "Oh, Dr. Libertino, I am so sorry. I can see you are on your way out and…"

Lila interrupted him, "Yes, Jeff. I am in a terrible hurry. Can this possibly wait till I return?"

Gloria stepped in front of Jeff and said in a rather curt, frosty tone, "This really cannot possibly wait, Lila, and I think you need to hear this now."

Lila sighed. Never, ever could she make a simple exit.

"Okay, you two. How about you walk me to my car and we can carry on this conversation on the way?"

Jeff, his large figure twisted slowly as he tried to maneuver his body around the hallway in the direction of the door.

Gloria had no trouble at all as she eagerly rushed on the heels of Lila.

"Yes, Gloria. What is it that is so urgent?"

"Well, Lila." Gloria had always called her Lila except when they were in front of others in a meeting. She seemed to think that her position gave her the professional right to call her principal by her first name. Lila just ignored her for the most part but did look sincerely at Gloria impatiently waiting for her to continue.

"You see, Lilar," Gloria's thick New York accent had Lila's name come across as Lilar and it made Lila stiffen to hear it.

"Yes, go on."

"It's one of our students. Her name is Cindy Newport. Her mother is being transferred to hospice at the moment and I'm afraid we need to find Cindy and get her to her mother. The hospital notified me because they couldn't locate Cindy and did not want her to miss seeing her mother at this most crucial time."

Lila stopped in her tracks. This was, indeed, quite serious. "Gloria, did you look on Cindy's information sheet to see who her emergency contact is? Who is her family? Her father? Any relatives?'

Gloria was mentally formulating her response as Jeff finally caught up with them in the parking lot, his breathing ragged and short. Both women looked at Jeff with concern. Lila made a mental note to have a courageous conversation with Jeff when she returned. He needed to see his doctor and get on some program, Weight Watchers or something. His face was red and he was bent over, his hands resting on his knees. She knew Jeff did not want any additional attention brought to him so she put this in the back of her mind for later.

Gloria waited until Lila was focusing on her again. "You see, Lila, she has no father, no relatives listed at all. Only Riley Maddox's mother, Dr. Jeanine Maddox, is her only emergency contact."

"Okay, Gloria," Lila expressed very slowly. "Call Dr. Maddox and explain the situation. Her daughter, Riley, is a good friend of Cindy's and she must know where she is for the summer. Let me know as soon as you know. You have my personal cell, correct?"

"Yes, ma'am. I do. I will notify you immediately. Thanks, Lila."

And with that, Gloria turned around and started walking briskly back to the building. Suddenly, she came to an abrupt halt, turned around, and waited patiently for Jeff.

Jeff walked slowly, his labored breathing audible even in the parking lot. Gloria, her short pumps clicking on the pavement made a beeline for him and grabbed his arm.

"Jesus, Jeff, you old fart, you really need to lose some weight and see a doctor ASAP, my friend."

Jeff, his balding head shiny with sweat beads, looked rather pasty and clammy. "I…uh…I…can't catch… my……breath."

"Okay," said Gloria, soothingly. "Take it slow. In and

out, 1,2,3. Okay, again. That's good. Now, let's get you into the air-conditioned building and get you some water."

Jeff could only nod and allowed Gloria to guide him little by little through the parking lot.

Cassandra, seeing the two of them walking so slowly back into the building, immediately ran to the office refrigerator grabbed a bottle of water, and soaked a paper towel. She opened the office door and the two of them staggered into the main office. Gloria steered Jeff onto the couch where he slumped over. Cassandra quickly handed him the bottle of water and a cool wet paper towel which she pressed on his sweat-soaked neck.

Cassandra looked anxiously at Gloria and asked, "Do I need to call 911?"

Gloria shook her head no and watched over Jeff as he sipped the bottle of water.

After ten minutes or so, Jeff seemed to be breathing normally again and he looked at both women and said softly, "God bless you both. I guess I'm falling apart. I… don't…take…very good care…of myself."

Gloria smiled. "Well, honey, you got two women who are going to be pecking at you every day until we see that you went to your doctor and are doing something positive about your body and your health. And that was not a request, got it, big guy?"

Jeff smiled while Cassandra was chuckling to herself. Gloria could be a bit aggressive at times, but those small brown eyes were absolutely filled with love and concern.

The three of them sat quietly together talking and joking as Jeff slowly recuperated.

• • •

Lila was not sure exactly what took place between Gloria and Jeff in the parking lot, but she knew she would be filled in as soon as she returned. In the meantime, she left the parking lot and called Darrius.

"Okay, Darrius, babe, I left school. Now, tell me what's up."

Darrius was out of breath as he spoke with her. "Honey, I'm at the hospital with Ben and…"

Before he could finish his sentence, Lila broke in with, "What do you mean? Ben! Is he hurt?"

"No, baby. It's not about Benjamin. Let me finish. He is at the hospital with his girlfriend, Meadow. She was throwing up violently. Ben confided in me. He thinks she is pregnant."

CHAPTER 14

Cindy was singing to Ariel, the golden Palomino. Cindy loved all the horses, but Ariel was her favorite. It didn't matter what Cindy was singing even though it tended to be the same Taylor Swift song over and over. As long as Ariel was being brushed, her dark mahogany eyes glazed over and her massive body shifted ever so slightly from side to side in accord with Cindy's rhythm.

"Ahhh, Ariel, I wish I could really sing like Taylor Swift, but you are stuck with me because 'Can't you see that I'm the one who understands you?'" sang Cindy, "and that's okay because you are truly the most gentlest horse I have ever known and I have known, well, you are the only horse I have ever known!" Cindy laughed to herself. She was alone in the stable if you consider five horses and Cindy was all alone. But she loved it. She could sing, talk, joke, even cry to any of the horses and none of them ever laughed at her.

Cindy gently rubbed the white star on Ariel's muzzle; it was as soft as a snowflake. She put both her hands on Ariel's head and pulled it towards her and tenderly kissed the marking. "I love you, Ariel. I wish I could stay with you always. I wish I could bring my mother here to meet you. I wish…I wish…"

And then Cindy allowed herself the time to cry. She had not cried in a long time, but thinking about her mother and the possibility that she might never see her again brought a rush of sudden tears.

"Damn the cancer!" Cindy whispered out loud. She did not want to scare Ariel or any of the other horses with her sudden outbursts, so she controlled her vocal explosion. But she was scared. She had not heard from her mother in a few weeks, and she looked forward to her letters. Cindy wrote to her mother every day, but she knew her mom was not able to return the letters as frequently. In fact, the last two letters she received were a few weeks ago and Cindy could tell that they were written by her mom's nurse. Cindy sobbed, tears flowing freely down her puffed cheeks, her chest hurting from the pounding of her heart. She knew that was not a good sign if her mom was not able to hold a pen to write her a letter.

Cindy heard the footsteps and the giggles before she saw the girls. Cindy loved her little trio of girls who she was in charge of this summer. Anika, Coby and Jasmine. Billy, the director of the camp, knew this was Cindy's first foray into being a camp counselor so he made sure she was in charge of only a few girls. Cindy's teacher, Mrs.

Waverly, was instrumental in finding her this summer job. She knew Billy from a long time ago, and she had asked him if there was room in his summer camp for Cindy to join and help out.

Cindy smiled, quickly wiping her eyes and her running nose as the three girls waltzed in oblivious to their surroundings until they saw their favorite counselor. With shrieks of joy, they ran over to her.

"Cindy, Cindy, Cindy!" cried Anika. Her long braids were flying in the air as she hurled into Cindy's welcoming stance. Cindy's loud 'oooof' did not deter little Anika from jumping on Cindy. Cindy caught Anika easily as she was the lightest of the group. Her twinkling blue eyes were slanted upwards and filled with so much love.

"Oh, my, Anika, you little goof! Let me let you down now so we can get our horses ready!"

Jasmine, shy and reticent, her long black hair tied back with a bright red scrunchie, and her tongue, sticking out as always, reached cautiously for Cindy's hands. Cindy spread her arms wide and pulled Jasmine in for her daily hug. Jasmine squealed with delight, her deep brown eyes that slanted upward were staring right into Cindy's face. Cindy held her tight, knowing that this interaction helped calm Jasmine and allowed her to follow whatever Cindy instructed.

Coby held back. She always did. Her cropped strawberry blond hair with long bangs that covered her light green eyes gave her the security of hiding. She was withdrawn, she stuttered when she was nervous, and her autism was only obvious when she was urged to interact with the others. Sometimes she looked at Cindy, but often times she stared into the distance, and Cindy would gently coax her back into the fold with soft, nurturing words that were non-threatening.

Cindy, before working at Billy's camp, had never been exposed so closely to kids with special needs. She may have seen them at school, but they were always in a different hallway with so many adults surrounding them that she never was in the same classroom setting. Cindy was never rude; it was simply that these students rarely interacted with the general education classes if their disabilities were too severe.

Before she started camp, Mrs. Waverly took her to Starbucks one day when school was over for the summer vacation. "Cindy," Neva began slowly, carefully choosing her words. "Cindy, I am very excited that you want to spend the summer working for my friend Billy. But I have to tell you something. Billy's camp is not the regular run-of-the-mill summer camp."

Cindy gazed at Mrs. Waverly praying that she was not going to be told the camp was an impossibility and that she had to prepare herself for a major letdown. She knew it. Just when she thought something good was about to happen in her life, well, damn, if something got in the way and completely send her for a loss. For a moment she figured that her chance to be a camp counselor was off the table and she would have to spend the entire summer alone while her mother was at a special cancer clinic receiving her treatments.

"It's okay, Mrs. Waverly," whispered Cindy, too afraid to speak up for fear her dreams were about to be dashed. "I'll be okay if I don't get to go to your friend's camp this summer. I'll…I'll…find something…"

Mrs. Waverly interrupted Cindy before she could finish. "Oh, no, my dear," she quickly spoke out. "Oh, no, sweetheart, you are definitely going to Billy's camp, and you are most assuredly going to be a camp counselor. You will probably be the best camp counselor Billy has ever had at the camp!"

Cindy's entire demeanor suddenly changed. She sat up a little higher and her smile was so large her cheeks hurt. "For real, Mrs. Waverly? You mean I am really going to the camp, for real? I thought you were about to tell me that…"

Neva stopped her right there. "No, my girl, I would never take back this offer. I only thought that you and I should have a talk about the kinds of girls you are going to be working with this summer."

Cindy looked confused. She turned her head from one side to the other. "I don't get you."

"Cindy, the girls at the camp all have special needs. Do you know what that means?"

Cindy scrunched her nose and pushed back her glasses. "You mean they can't talk or see and they're all in wheelchairs or something like that?"

Neva took a deep breath. She realized that so many

students had no understanding of what a special needs child meant in relationship to other kids. Kids today rely on what others tell them, and what they learn on social media or from movies. Unless a student had a sibling or a cousin or even a neighbor with special needs, they were, well, clueless.

"Cindy," Neva began slowly. "I'm going to explain what special needs in another student means and how you, my dear, are going to be able to work with the girls and help them oh so much this summer."

Cindy's smile only grew larger, her eyes lit up and she took a quick gulp of the caramel frappe Mrs. Waverly had purchased for her. "Tell me, Mrs. Waverly, tell me everything I need to know."

And so for the next few hours, as the two of them sat sipping their favorite coffee frappes, Mrs. Waverly shared all that she knew about special needs kids.

• • •

The three girls, filled with anticipation, waited anxiously for Cindy to tell them what to do.

Anika spoke first. "Can we go on the horshtttt now, Chindy?" Cindy smiled. Mrs. Waverly had informed her about certain speech issues and Cindy knew exactly what Anika was saying to her. "I wanna go first, Chindy, cause Coby is a doody head and she always goes first."

Cindy took a deep breath and said soothingly, "Anika, Coby is not a doody head. And besides, today is your day to do first, so come here and let me get you up on your horse."

Jasmine started to cry. She cried easily especially when she didn't get her way. Cindy thought that maybe she always got her way at home and it was difficult for her to be patient.

Jasmine's gentle sobs escalated into loud bawling, "Anika's gonna get in trouble, Miss Cindy, cause she called Coby a name. She's in big, big trouble."

"No, I'm not," interrupted Anika. "I'm a good girl so you can't say that."

Cindy sighed. She had lots of patience with the girls, but some days it took all of it just to get the girls corralled onto their horses and they hadn't even left the stable yet.

Coby jumped right into the conversation and as usual, she was starting something completely non sequitur so Cindy could never think of what to add to the chatter.

"My dad is working on the farm back home and we are going to grow corn," Coby interjected.

Cindy quickly answered, "Coby, that's great. Now how about I get you up on your horse?"

Coby nodded, ignoring the arguing that Anika and Jasmine were having around her, and quickly grabbed onto the reins of her horse allowing Cindy to hoist her up.

It seemed like forever, but Cindy managed to get all three girls on their horses.

Billy shared with her that he managed to keep the gentlest horses he knew. They were called quarter horses, he had explained to her. They were to easiest to work with.

And before she knew it, Billy was spending the next hour sharing everything he knew about quarter horses from their origins in Kentucky to Texas to the Carolinas. It was a bit too much for Cindy to process it all. She was okay with just feeling safe knowing that the three horses the girls were on were not going to start racing for the woods.

"Okay, girls. Now follow me closely and do not ride ahead of me. I will lead the way and we are going to have a wonderful ride this morning. Are you all ready?" Cindy hoisted herself onto Ariel and turned around to find Anika, Jasmine, and Coby all lined up perfectly ready to follow.

"Good job, everyone. Now here we go." And with that, Cindy gently nudged Ariel to walk out of the stable with the girls in tow.

The day was beautiful. The trees were lush with green leaves, the sky was a clear blue, and the grass was soft and lush under the horses' hooves as they made their way to the trail. The trail would take them on an hour loop and somewhere in the middle of their journey they would stop and have sandwiches and drinks that Cindy had secretly packed in her saddle bags.

Cindy loved this part of the day. The girls behind her giggled and shouted in glee whenever a bird flew close to them or a butterfly landed on the horse's mane. Nothing could go wrong, thought Cindy. Nothing.

They were close to the halfway mark to stop and enjoy their snacks when Billy came riding behind them. He had a serious look on his face and there was sweat dripping down his temples as though he had been riding fast and hard.

Cindy was confused. Billy never showed up on her riding trips. A slow chill in the pit of her stomach grew and her hands slipped off her reins from sweat.

Billy pulled up his reins and slowed down his horse. King was a huge quarter horse, all black, and stood a huge 18 hands tall. Billy reached his hands onto the neck of King and said softly, "Whoa, boy. Slow down. I need you to hold it here. Good boy."

And with that, Billy slid off King, tied the reins to a nearby bush, and trotted over to Cindy.

"Hi, Cindy. Look, I know you are on your morning hike with the girls, but you have a visitor back at the ranch and I think you need to go see her. Like now. It's okay, I'll take over for you." And with that, he looked over at the girls and smiled. "Hey, Anika, Jasmine and Coby. You three are looking absolutely wonderful on top of your horses. Can you name them for me?"

The girls laughed loudly which was typical, but Cindy didn't hear a thing. She turned her horse back towards the ranch, dug her heels into the sides of Ariel, and in a strong commanding voice shouted, "Let's go, Ariel. Hyup, hyup, here we go."

Cindy did not look back. She knew Billy was in charge and she felt safe and assured about that. What she didn't feel good about was who was coming to visit her and more importantly…why?

CHAPTER 15

Lucas and Angelo, his dad, were on their annual fishing trip at their cabin. The sky was a clear blue and the trees were full and lush, not that Lucas cared about his surroundings. He couldn't wait till he had his rod in the river. There was nothing like fishing in the river because the fish would bite at any type of bait he threw out there and the exhilaration of pulling in that huge bass was better than anything he had experienced.

But the more Lucas tried to recall that memory, the more it grew blurry and so hazy he could barely make out the scenes. More and more vignettes of the two of them came rushing into his head like a wave crashing over him, but the images shattered into darker, more sinister shapes. He couldn't place it exactly, but his skin prickled as his father's hand massaged his back and slipped lower and lower until…

"Lucas, you okay, son?" Walter asked. "I thought I lost you there for a minute while I was talking about the football season with the new NFL coach and…and…man, Lucas, what's up, man?"

Lucas's soft blue eyes had glazed over. He shook his head violently from side to side as though it were one of the old toys his grandfather had shown him, an etch-a-something or other, that erased the image once you shook the gadget. He could hear Walter in the background talking but it sounded garbled like he was underwater. Lucas thought he was drowning, sucked in the air violently, and coughed hard until his throat burned.

Walter pulled off the road into the local grocery store, stopped the car, shut off the engine, and turned to look at Lucas. He could see the sheen of sweat on Lucas's forehead and his skin was pale and pasty. It immediately made Walter think back to that horrific time he found Lucas that one cold night in the elementary school playground huddled in the old playhouse shivering and shaking as though he were living in a nightmare. The custodian of the school had found Lucas hiding back there and because Walter was on patrol that night, he had answered the call from the school.

Walter remembered the fear in Lucas's eyes, and it took a long time before he could convince Lucas to come out. He had tossed Lucas a blanket and Paul, the custodian, had brought him some hot chocolate that he had made for Lucas back in the building. Walter was shocked that Lucas stretched out his quivering hand to Walter to accept the drink. Lucas took the steaming cup, trembling like a leaf in a hurricane. As hot as the chocolate was, Lucas drank it as fast as he could and then sat there holding onto the warm mug while he covered himself in the blanket.

And now, staring at Lucas, he saw that same look of terror that had draped over Lucas like a dark wool blanket of evil. What was he seeing in his young mind that caused him to shrink into a shadowy hole filled with a gruesome nightmarish trauma?

Walter reached over to touch Lucas gently on his shoulder and Lucas screamed and coiled back into his car door as if Walter was a burning rod that was smoldering his skin. Walter yanked his arm back and whispered very softly, "Breathe, Lucas. It's okay, son. I'm here with you. It's Walter. It's Walter. No one else."

And the realization came to Walter, like a burst dam flooding his memory with the heinous and disgusting visions that Lucas had shared about his father touching him. Touching him not like a daddy hugs his child, but a sickened adult who should never have been around children – ever.

Walter felt inadequate and incapable of pulling Lucas out of his hell. He and Lucas's mom, Julie, had spoken with Miss Anna. She was Lucas's therapist and had given Walter and Julie some guidelines on how to deal with Lucas when he slipped into his abyss and could not climb out. Anna was not legally allowed to share the stories that Lucas had in confidence told her, but Julie and Walter knew enough from what Lucas had told the police when Angelo, Lucas's biological father, was arrested.

Walter took a slow, deep breath and stared into Lucas's

eyes. They were still glazed, but Walter was not going to give up.

"Lucas, it's me, Walter. Your dad is not here. He is nowhere near here. He is locked up in jail far, far away, son."

Lucas turned his head, his brown hair falling into his eyes. He appeared to be listening, but not quite comprehending. Not yet. Walter felt like he had just pried open the heavy door. He did not want that door to slam shut again, so he kept talking all the while hearing Anna's words in the back of his head.

"Go slow," she had advised. "Talk gently and easily and don't make any sudden moves towards him. He needs to feel his space is safe. You cannot burst that bubble. Keep talking. About anything, especially things he likes and feels comfortable about. His friends, sports, even food…just don't reach out to him until he comes to you."

And with those words in his thoughts, Walter continued, "Hey, Lucas. We are almost at the cabin. I want to show you how to start a fire in the pit around the back of the cabin. I brought some hot dogs with me, and we can roast them and I even brought the stuff you love to make s'mores.

"You know, chocolate and graham crackers and marshmallows. It's going to be a good time. I know it's cold outside, but remember how much you love those summer nights that are just beginning to get a bit cold?"

Lucas blinked. And blinked again and then rubbed his eyes. He moaned a deep sound that came from far down inside him that made Walter tear up. It was a sound like a wounded animal who was hurting so badly it could not stop itself from whimpering.

Walter wanted to hug him and squeeze the heinous nightmare out of his soul, but he knew he couldn't do it. Not yet. Not with the awful memory of his father still clawing at his inner psyche with nails that were ripping his insides to shreds.

Lucas pulled his knees up to his chest and hugged his knees as though they were the medicine he needed. Walter had another flashback of Lucas doing the exact same thing that frightful night in the school playhouse.

"I...I..." Lucas was trying to put words together, but they were stuck in his throat.

Lucas's head slumped onto his knees and Walter could see his shoulders moving up and down and knew that Lucas was crying silently. But that was a good thing. Anna had explained that the crying was a sign that Lucas was coming out of his vision, slowly at first, and the tears were the first sign that he was pushing the episode away.

Walter slid over just the smallest of movements. His large, calloused hands were reaching out towards Lucas, cautiously, expectantly, hoping against hope that Lucas would not slide back into his personal hell again.

Lucas lifted his head, his eyes rimmed with tears, his nose red and dripping.

"I hate him! I hate what he did to me! I never, ever want to see him again! But, Jesus, Walter, why do I have to relive those?" Lucas sobbed, his words getting swallowed in his tears.

Now Walther knew he could move closer. He reached for Lucas and Lucas collapsed into his arms.

"Shhhhh, son, it's okay. I'm here and I will never let him hurt you ever again. You are safe with me, and I will protect you. Do you hear me? I mean it, Lucas. You will never have to worry about him. I promise you."

Lucas allowed himself to be enveloped by Walter. His strong shoulders braced Lucas, and he pressed his face hard against Walter's chest, the tears flowing freely down his face. He was not embarrassed; he was not holding back. He had always known Walter was his protector but for so long he could not allow himself the freedom to let him in. He used the color of Walter's skin as a shield to keep him away.

Lucas hiccupped, his crying subsided and he pulled back from Walter. He wiped his nose on the back of his arm and looked into Walter's deep brown eyes.

"I…uh…I don't know what to say. I don't know how to thank you. I know you're the good guy. I just…I don't know…it's so hard for me to accept…to forget him and know that you and Mom are there for me.

"Sometimes, something…I don't know what…just something sets me off, sets off a memory and I feel like I'm falling, falling fast and hard and I can't stop it, Walter. I can't. I told Miss Anna about this, and she keeps telling me it will take time for those dreams to fade. They scare the hell outta me and I don't want them to happen. I want to be myself again, Walter, but I don't know how."

Walter nodded, and he smiled. "You remember when you fell off your skateboard about a month ago and it was bleeding real bad?" Lucas nodded, not sure where this was going.

Walter continued, "And I put on a bandage for a couple of days and when I took off the bandage, it bled again like a stuck pig. Well, once the bleeding stopped and we let it dry out and it scabbed over you thought it was all good and done. And then you tripped over your damn cleats in the hallway and that knee started squirting blood all over again. Remember?"

Lucas nodded again, still puzzled.

"Well, son. What your father did to you was the most awful thing in the world. But with time, your heart will heal, and those memories will scab over. But sadly, every now and again they will get torn open, and they will bleed something awful. But, Lucas, man, I promise you, it will not destroy you, it will not define you and it will certainly not make you hate everyone and everything around you.

"Just know that your mom and me are here for you. We will always be here for you and when that damn scab bursts open again, we will help you seal it up no matter how many times it gets ripped apart. The more we work together to sew it up, the stronger it will become and the harder it will be for it to tear open again. You hear me?"

For the first time in a very long time, Lucas looked at Walter with a new understanding, an epiphany, and he smiled. A huge smile.

Lucas leaned over and hugged Walter hard. "Thanks, Walter. Hey, how soon till we can eat those dogs cause I'm really hungry!"

Walter let out a belly laugh and started the car. "We are almost there, my man…almost there!"

CHAPTER 16

Cindy rode Ariel in a gentle jog all the way back to the stables. She wasn't expecting anyone, and it was a bit uncomfortable. "Who is coming to see me, girl?" she asked Ariel, knowing quite well that her horse was not going to respond. Her beautiful mane was swinging in the wind, but an answer was not forthcoming.

Cindy wanted to push Ariel to her limits and have her gallop, but while galloping was the most fun ever, Cindy secretly felt compelled to slow down as though the longer it took to see who was waiting for her, the better. "If it's good news, well, Ariel, then we will certainly have a great night, but oh, God, do you think it's about my mom? No, she's okay. She has to be okay. I mean, I haven't heard from her in a while, but that's because the chemo makes her so tired."

Ariel snorted as though she was agreeing with Cindy, but the closer Cindy rode to the ranch, the more her nerves unraveled. And then her heart started racing and her hands tingled as she held the reins.

"Stop it! Stop it, I said. Right now! I will not fall apart on me. I won't have it! I have come too far and I'm not the same scared girl I was back home! Stop it!" Cindy's hands gripped the reins tighter even as they shook uncontrollably.

She breathed in slowly and started counting out loud to Ariel which made her feel less silly about working on her anxiety therapy. "Okay, Ariel, count with me, girl-friend… And it's one, two, three and four. Breathe out. And it's one, two, three and four. Good girl, you're doing just fine. Stay with me now. Breathe in slowly and hold." Cindy controlled her breath as her head bobbed up and down counting. The trees blurred by and although she was riding on the main trail back to the ranch, Cindy prayed that her horse would not deviate from the path since she was allowing Ariel to guide herself.

Cindy was oblivious of the time. It usually took a good thirty minutes from the ranch to the area where Cindy had taken her three girls. But now, on the way back, between worrying about who was waiting for her along with the onset of an anxiety attack, Cindy had lost track of time. She tried observing the landscapes around her that would alert her to where she was on the trail.

And then she saw it. It was the beautiful magnolia tree off the path standing in all its glory. The star-shaped flow-ers were blooming in bursts of purple and yellow. The tree always made her smile and think of her mother. She and her mom had traveled down south one spring break a few years ago and they had a picnic in a beautiful little park that was outlined with huge magnolia trees. Her mom even made her get up from their blanket and walk over to one of the trees and hug it! Mom had laughed and told her she was an official tree hugger and from now on she was the keeper of all the magnolia trees in the land.

Cindy's eyes welled up with tears thinking about that beautiful memory. But she also knew how close she was to the ranch and so she nudged Ariel with her thighs to go a bit faster. Cindy was breathing normally now. The first noticeable sign was her hands. They were no longer tingling. The reins were relaxed in her hands and her chest was no longer heaving in and out. Her forehead was drenched in sweat, but she didn't care. The attack was sudden, but she felt pride in her ability to overcome those horrible sensations of losing control. She whispered to Ariel, "I can thank Miss Anna for that! Oh, yes, indeed. She is my hero, and I will write to her tonight and tell her how strong I am. Of course, Ariel, you did help!" And with that, Cindy giggled to herself.

Seeing the ranch farther down the trail, Cindy sat up as tall as she could in her saddle and urged Ariel on with more intensity.

And as Cindy approached the stables, she saw the car. She recognized it immediately and her heart sank. It was Riley's car. Well, her parents' car. And why would they be here? It wasn't visitation day and Cindy still had two weeks left in the camp before it was time to return home. And where were they? They must have been in the main house since Cindy did not see anyone around the stables or the car. Again, she thought to herself – what were they doing here and am I going home now?

Home. Which home? Her home? Riley's home? Ariel slowed down to a walk as though she were reading Cindy's hesitation. She snorted and stomped her feet. Cindy dismounted and grabbing the reins gently, guided Ariel into her stall. Cindy carefully eased Ariel's saddle off her back. Once the saddle was nestled on the wooden holder, Cindy picked up the wooden brush and stroked Ariel's back. She was stalling and she knew it. She rationalized that it was necessary to always cool down your horse, but then again, one of her girls could have done that for her. Why was she delaying going to the main house? Because she knew it wasn't good news. People did not come up to the camp with good news and then return home. And her mother always told her that bad news can wait since it will always be there waiting to pounce on you.

Cindy put back the brush on the shelf and then grabbed the worn handle hoof pick. She leaned her body into Ariel so she could lift her foot and scoop out the mud and debris in her metal shoe. Cindy repeated this procedure for each leg, slowly, deliberately knowing that each passing moment was only bringing her closer to a situation that she felt was not going to end well.

She hung up the hoof pick and went back to Ariel, holding her muzzle in both her hands and kissing her above her soft lips. "You be a good girl and if I'm not back here tomorrow I promise I will see you again." Cindy choked and swallowed hard. She kissed Ariel one more time, breathed in the aroma of hay and horse and wood, and then closed her stable door. Cindy did not look back. It was too painful.

The main house was located past the stables and closer to the apple orchard that Billy had planted years ago. The front door was open, and the metal crossings on the screen door glowed with the reflection of the kitchen lights. Cindy heard voices but did not recognize who they were at first.

Cindy walked up the old cracked wooden porch steps slowly, dreading the reality of what was going to happen next. She stood at the screen door for a moment, took a deep breath, and held it. She shook her head from side to side and said to herself, *Grow up, Cin…deal with whatever is beyond this door. Now go!*

She pulled the screen door wide open and stepped inside.

Riley turned to face her; her amber eyes swollen from crying. Riley never cries, thought Cindy. And her short brown hair was now shoulder length. She looked so different from just a month ago.

"Cin," Riley whispered, and she took a step towards her. Behind her, Cindy now saw Riley's parents, Jeanine and Gunther, both doctors. They never took time off and yet they were both here…now. The hair on Cindy's neck stood straight up and she felt chills run up and down her body.

"Riley…uh Doctor and uh…doctor? Why? Ummmm, what's going on? You're all here?"

Jeanine stepped forward, her silver hair loose along her shoulders. She reached Cindy and gently took her in her arms, her dove-gray eyes wet with tears.

"Cindy, honey. Riley and her dad and I came up here because, well, baby…it's your mom. We need you to come home with us so you can see your mom, before…well, let Riley help you pack your things and we'll take you back with us now. Okay, baby?"

Cindy froze. "Is…she…dead?" Cindy said the words methodically, coldly because this was not the time to fall apart. She needed to brace herself. She needed to be strong. For her mother.

Riley's father stepped forward. Cindy hardly ever saw Riley's father. He was the male version of Riley with the same color hair and eyes except he was tall. So tall it made Cindy feel tiny, insignificant.

"Cindy, I don't mean to rush you, but time is of the essence. Your mother is not well, and she is very weak, and she has asked to see you as soon as we can bring you. So, Riley, take Cindy to her bunkhouse if you don't mind, and see whatever you can pack. If we cannot get it all, we will return at another time and finish whatever is necessary."

Riley took Cindy's hand and walked her out of the kitchen knowing that Cindy was not processing everything that was happening, but she needed to get her moving quickly.

Gunther reached for Jeanine's hand while they were left alone in the kitchen.

He looked at his wife and said softly, "I wish we could have done more for Mattie. I wish we could have saved her."

Jeanine nodded, leaning into her husband. "I wish we could save Cindy from today and all of her tomorrows."

CHAPTER 17

Shaynee sat at her favorite chair at Starbucks staring at her Caramel Ribbon Crunch Frappuccino. She was playing with the straw but not tasting her drink. Her dark amber eyes were fixed on the front door, waiting.

"Where are you, butthead?" Shaynee questioned out loud and then quickly turned around to see if anyone had heard her. Just as she looked back at her drink, she heard him come through the door.

"Gee, Cuz, what's the 911 for? I mean I was busy with a new girl I had just met and you definitely cooled the hot shocks that I was delivering!" Stetson's arched eyebrows were scrunched up high in his forehead as he swooped in and plopped himself right across from Shaynee. Without so much as a "sorryboutbeinglateIgotbusy" excuse that he usually said, he eagerly snatched the frappe from Shaynee and began slurping down the sweet drink.

"Ow, I think I just got myself a Slurpee headache from that, what is that?" Stetson asked.

Shaynee smiled. She loved Stetson even when he acted like such a jerk. He was her cousin and best friend and there were no secrets between them and now…well…now she had to share something that was going to blow his mind. It had already exploded inside her beyond her wildest imagination and she was still struggling with coming to grips with her incredulous information.

"Hello, Stetson," she said casually. She did not want to come on too strong too urgent or too excited. He would fail to see the seriousness of the situation, so she took her time.

Stetson ignored her welcome and continued to suck the straw as hard as he could almost draining the cup. Shaynee stared at his ability to completely block out anything around him when it came to eating or drinking something he liked.

Shaynee waited for Stetson to finish the frappe he had absconded from her knowing that if she ordered another one he would just drink that one also. She would get one, or rather two, in a few minutes. She needed to talk and get it out before she got cold feet and ran out the door never to divulge the greatest secret she had in the entire world. And that was a very real possibility as the weightiness of what she was about to share unnerved her.

Shaynee smiled. She adored her cousin to the max, always had even when they were little and he was such a tease. He loved to pull her hair just to hear her scream at him, loved to tug her shorts down in public because, well, he had said that was such a cool thing to do. Shaynee learned to wear yoga shorts under all her clothes and to make sure her hair was tightly fastened until Stetson finally grew out of those immature pranks.

"You know how much I love you, Stetson," Shaynee began.

"Yeah, you love me like a brother you always said," Stetson expressed, his lips still sucking at the crunchy caramel pieces on the bottom of the drink making all kinds of slurping noises. "So what up? Why am I here and not with my new number?"

"Yes, I do love you like you were my brother but you are my favorite cuz," Shaynee started.

"Uh, I believe I'm your only cuz, Cuz," Stetson hit back with a smirk. "Oooh, wait a sec," he laughed. "I can't leave Colton and Cameron out, now can I? Ya know, you are very lucky to have little bros around the house. And I enjoy teasing them more than when I teased you. Ya know why? Because they are too little to know I'm making fun of them and I love it!"

"Hahahah," Shaynee forced a laugh. "You should be so lucky to be an only child cause you never have the responsibility of babysitting or getting in trouble for something those boys did but I get blamed for doing it just because I'm the older sibling.

"Okay, enough stupid talk," she continued and then coughed to clear her throat. "Here goes, and please, no interrupting until I am done. Is that clear?"

"Crystal," he cooed and winked at her as though he was worshipping her every word.

"So…do you remember when we were sitting at the bench table at lunchtime when Riley came up to us and started teasing us about being so secretive, blah, blah, blah?"

Stetson looked up, quizzically. "You mean back at school before ol' BA came and yelled at us? Yeah…So?"

"Did I not tell you to wait until I was done talking and to not interrupt me and no, do not answer me right now – that was a rhetorical question."

"A what? Oh, damn, sorry. Go on."

"Anyway," Shaynee followed more determinedly. Riley left her group at lunch and busted into our private conversation that we were having. Remember, I said it was private – between you and me because I had something to tell you. Then Riley split my world apart and said that she had a sneaking suspicion that you and I weren't cousins at all, but that we were twins. Hello, Stetson! Drop the mike, here, dude."

Stetson opened his mouth and was about to say something but the look on Shaynee's face sliced him in two and he clamped his mouth shut.

"So, after we were eating lunch, I forced you to spit into a clean cup. You thought I was being stupid or something, but trust me, I knew exactly what I was doing. I took your…uhh…spit and dripped it into a special vial and mailed it away to be tested for DNA."

Shaynee saw the look of confusion on Stetson's face and immediately she snapped, "DON'T ASK! At least not yet."

Shaynee blew out her breath slowly, and cautiously. She looked around to see if anyone was dipping into their conversation. It was a small town and gossip flew around like a tornado in the movie, *Twister.* "Did it never occur to you that you and I look exactly alike and, yeah, I know cousins can share a lot of their DNA, but then, and I'm sorry if I'm rambling here, but Stets, I got to get this all out or I'm gonna bust. I swear I'm gonna fall apart so let me keep going.

"It all started when I took a good long look at my dad. You know Uncle Bryant is a sweetheart to you and I love him, but I look absolutely and positively nothing like him. Not a hair on my body connects me to my dad. He's blonde, I'm not. He has dark hazel eyes, you and me both have amber-colored eyes. And his nose. Forget it. You and me, Stets– we both have those rather large and sorry, ugly big noses. And then the kicker – my brothers. My twin brothers, Colton and Cameron? They look like a combo of mom and dad."

Stetson was bursting at the seams, fidgeting in his chair, the straw hanging recklessly from his dried lips. Shaynee knew she had to give him a chance to say something even if it was a short one. She stalled. She stuttered. She coughed. She was afraid to let him say anything for fear of, well, she wasn't sure what was going to happen. This was the tipping point and there was no going back now. There would never be a *howsitgoingcuz* conversation again. Shaynee froze. There might never be any conversation between the two of them ever again because from this moment till the day they both left the physical world, well, life would never be the same for them. Ever again.

"Shayz," he busted out, "Where the hell are you going here? You never told me about some NDA testing or something. What are you trying to prove?"

"Idiot," she chuckled, "It's DNA testing and that stands for DNA or deoxyribonucleic acid. It's the stuff that is in our body, human bodies, and well when another human has the same levels of this stuff that means there is a connection. And not a coinky-dink connection – a real, live connection like we could be more than just cousins."

"I'm good with us being just cousins. Why do you want more? We're not going to change who we are or nothing. Why did you have to go and change the world?" Stetson was angry. His breath was sharp and ragged and his eyes glistened. His throat tightened.

"I liked who we were. I love that you and I are so close because we are cousins. Why did you have to go and fu… screw it all up? And shit, does that mean I do have a father? Wait! Wait a damn minute now! Are you saying we have the same father?

"Oh, hell, Shay, what about our birthdays? We are nine months apart. Were. Whose birthday is the real one? Whose birthday is made up? I am so confused. My head is doing somersaults and I don't know who I am anymore."

Shaynee understood that Stetson never knew about a dad. He had always looked at her father, Bryant as a surrogate father. His mom, Brynley, had always said the father of her child had moved away before he was born and never came back.

Stetson was gagging. He was burping and gagging at

the table so Shaynee grabbed him by the arm and yanked him out of Starbucks leaving her new half-drunk cups rocking on the table.

Once outside, Stetson leaned over an empty parking space and heaved, large hunks of the frozen drink rushing out of his mouth. He coughed and hiccuped and wiped his mouth. He looked at Shaynee and spittle came flying out of his cracked lips, "Why did you have to ruin my life? Why did you have to tell me things that I can never go back from? I liked my life. I liked Uncle Bryant like he was my dad. And now you tell me there is a dad out there? And you're my real sister like we were born together? And which one is our real mom? Yours or mine? God, Shay, I have too many questions and I feel like my head is gonna bust wide open!"

Shaynee pulled Stetson away from his throw-up now gliding down to the sewer at the other end of the street and quietly guided him along the sidewalk to where there was an empty bench at the farthest end of the shopping center. She put her arm around Stetson and pulled him close to her. This was not going to be easy with Stetson.

"Stets, my dearest and closest friend, when I got your DNA results back – and mine, too, well, I started looking at my ancestry page. Yes, I signed up for that without our moms knowing about it. And here's the goddamn shocker. Get ready for this one, Stets."

Stetson stared into Shaynee's eyes and nodded cautiously afraid of what Shaynee was going to tell him. He closed his eyes, took a slow breath, crossed his chest, and whimpered, "Go on."

"We have an incredibly strong DNA connection with a man named Ronald Torres who lives in Puerto Rico. I looked him up."

Shaynee uncoiled her arm from Stetson's shoulder and plucked her cell phone from her back pocket. She clicked open her photo page and scrolled down to a picture. She stared at it for a minute and then turned the phone around so Stetson could see it.

"Now who the fuck do you think this man looks like, Stets?" Shaynee asked, her grip on her phone so tight her knuckles were getting pale from the loss of blood.

Stetson stared at the man in the photo, his eyes widening and his full lips opening up as the vision in front of him was like looking into the mirror and seeing himself. He shook his head from side to side.

"Holy shit!" he cried. "Who the hell is Ronald Torres?"

CHAPTER 18

arl was completely serene sleeping on the couch with Emma tucked in beside him and CC curled up next to Emma. Emma's curly brown hair was intertwined with CC's long auburn hair and if one looked too quickly at the two of them it was difficult to identify whose hair belonged to either CC or Emma. And of course, on the floor stretched out in deep slumber, the protector of the group, was Atticus. Atticus, when he was not with his owner, Neva, adored Emma and CC and just tolerated Carl. Carl accepted this relationship and only shared how much fun Atticus was having with the girls whenever he touched base with Neva.

The room was quiet except for some jazz music playing from Carl's phone. The front door opened slowly and softly and Chip, Carl's brother, quietly slipped in. Chip immediately assumed his group must have been in serious napping mode or shoveling mouthfuls of food into their bodies. Not even a barking sound from Atticus broke the silence.

Chip tiptoed into the living room and halted. Looking at his brother, his precious daughter, and Carl's girlfriend CC, Chip could not help but smile. He never had that relationship with Emma's mother, Tarynda, and it saddened him even more that Tam, as he used to call her, did not want anything to do with Emma. Looking at his daughter with a love so deep it made his chest hurt, Chip was thankful for having reconciled with Carl. Having Carl back in his life gave him the confidence to return to school and get his teaching degree. Once he completed all his requirements, he knew he would be able to afford child care for Emma and eventually get his own place and move on with his life. A life with just Emma and him. And to be honest, that was perfectly okay. At least for now. He was not looking for a replacement mother or a new girlfriend, no, he was content with the way things were.

Standing there and smiling to himself, Chip felt like an idiot. "And I would love to be napping right there next to all three of you," Chip said aloud.

Carl slowly pried his one brown eye open to see his younger brother rocking back and forth as though he were in holding baby mode. "Dude," Carl whispered, trying not to wake up Emma or CC.

Chip's lips curled into a crooked smile and his sky-blue eyes twinkled with tears.

Carl sat up just a bit and adjusted himself so that Emma

and CC fell back against the soft cushions and were not disturbed at all. Atticus finally sat up; his mouth opened and his canines glistened threateningly. Carl quickly placed his hand on the dog's thick-haired neck to communicate with him that Chip was okay to be there and not to eat him.

He looked at his brother and chuckled. "You are one goofy little brother, you know that?" Carl quipped. "You are standing there wavering back and forth and smiling all teary-eyed. You okay?"

"Oh, man, Carl, I am more than okay. Seeing you and Emma and that gorgeous girlfriend of yours. I just gotta ask you, bro," Chip finally sat down and then finished his thought. "Man, when are you gonna wake up and ask that incredible girlfriend of yours to marry you? Shit, she sat by your side through thick and thin, and if she is still here then she must have been either hit over the head or is a mile deep in love with you."

Carl nodded, but didn't know what to say and then suddenly, Cassandra moaned and stretched, and with curled lips she muttered, "What are you two boys busy talking about when you don't know nothing about nothing?" Cassandra giggled.

Carl was so smitten with Cassandra that sometimes he felt paralyzed in her presence. Staring at her intently he could not talk or move. And then much to his surprise, he sat up, slid off the couch, and on one knee turned to Cassandra and said, his throat husky and sputtering, "Cassandra Conway, I love you. I have loved you since the day I ran into the main office and stared into your deep chocolate eyes and melted like a damn chocolate candy bar. I love you more than life itself and…" Carl started choking. He turned around and looked at Chip who just grinned like a hyena and kept nodding his head up and down like a broken bobblehead.

Carl started again. He cleared his throat, and when he dug his hand deep into his pocket, Cassandra gasped. He pulled out a small velvet box.

"CC," he uttered, "I, Carl DeWitt, do declare my undying love for you now and forever and will to the best of my ability be the absolute best partner on this earth for you…if you will have me. Cassandra Conway, will you marry me?" A tear slid down Carl's cheek and he let it fall onto the hand that was holding the soft black velvet box.

Carl opened the box and Cassandra sucked in the air in front of her in disbelief. She ogled the most precious cut pear-shaped diamond she had ever seen.

"When? How? Carl DeWitt! Have I told you how much I love you?"

"Does that mean?"

"Oh, dear God, Yes, Carl, I will marry you, as your brother Chip is my witness and dear Emma is still sleeping, yes I will marry you and be by your side forever and always!"

Carl was laughing, Chip was guffawing, and CC was crying happy tears. Emma started rubbing her eyes and sat up and muttered, "Wh…what…is…g…g…going on here?"

Chip rushed over, scooped up his daughter, and hugged

her tight. "Oh, baby, CC is going to be your new aunt. She and Carl are going to get married and we will all be one big happy family!"

Emma squealed in delight! She clapped her hands, her sleepy eyes still only half opened, and declared, "I knew CC was going to be my mommy. I just knew it!"

Carl, Chip, and Cassandra all looked at each other, shrugged their shoulders, and said in unison, "Of course, sweetie!"

CHAPTER 19

Cindy stayed in the back seat with Riley. Both girls were silent and every now and then Riley reached over to take Cindy's hand, but Cindy pulled back. She did not want to be comforted; she did not want to be consoled; she wanted to hold her mom.

Cindy coughed and said, "Dr. Maddox, excuse me, but how much longer till we are there? Are we going straight to the hospital?"

Jeanine Maddox breathed in. She knew Cindy was talking to her and not to her husband. It wasn't personal; Cindy barely knew Gunther and that was okay. She wanted Cindy to be as calm as possible on this ride home because she knew that the worst was about to happen. Jeanine lived these traumas and unspeakably tragic events almost daily. It was not an easy part of her job, but it was an integral part of her daily life.

"Cindy, hon," Jeanine said softly, "Your mom was transferred from the hospital to a lovely home where she is very comfortable. She wants to see you, but I need to tell you…"

"That she's gonna die," Cindy burst in, her throat catching on the words. Cindy's dark blue eyes were filled with tears, and she could not hold them back any longer. She rubbed her nose with her forearm wiping the leakage that was running without stopping. Riley leaned over and handed her a bunch of tissues from the plastic storage holder behind the front seat. Cindy squeezed the handful of tissues into a ball and pressed them up onto her nostrils.

Jeanine sighed. This was so hard when dealing with young adults. They knew the outcome, but it never made it any easier. "Your mom, Cindy, is a real trooper. She has been undergoing chemotherapy for quite some time now, but…" Jeanine blew out some air before she continued. "But unfortunately, the meds have not been working for you Mom. I'm not sure why because, well, I won't go into that right now."

"How much…" Cindy faltered. She wiped her nose and then her eyes. She sat up as straight as she could in the seat, reached over for Riley's hand, and held it tightly. She needed the support, the comfort now. "How much time does my mom have, Dr. M.? Please tell me. I need to know. I…need…to…know."

Cindy was almost fifteen and she knew her mom was young, just in her thirties. She also knew that Delores, her grandmother, also died from cancer – young. They were both smokers. Cindy remembers crying when she was having her ten-year-old birthday party and when she blew out the candles her mother asked what she had wished for and Cindy told her she wished her mother would stop smoking. And Mattie did stop. For a while at least. Cindy could tell when her mother was stressed that she would go out in the backyard and smoke. Her mom tried to hide it from Cindy, but Cindy could always tell.

Cindy promised she would get a job to help with the bills, but Mattie would not let her. Mattie wanted Cindy to remain as young and carefree for as long as she could. When Mattie got pregnant at nineteen her easy-going days were definitely over. Not that she ever made Cindy feel bad; Mattie loved being a mom and she adored her daughter, but she had to quit college and go to work. But most importantly, Mattie never looked back. Not once.

Jeanine Maddox pulled into the driveway of a very large home. Cindy looked out her window and thought they were arriving at a museum or a castle.

"Are we here?" Cindy asked anxiously, her hand automatically pushing up bangs that were no longer there anymore because her hair had grown so much these past few months. A nervous habit that Cindy did not realize she was doing.

Jeanine put the car into park, shut off the ignition, and turned around to face Cindy.

"Cindy," murmured delicately, "Your mom is very, very weak, and tired. She might not recognize you at first and she might not even be able to open her eyes.

"Do you want me to come in with you, dear?" Jeanine was treading very gently because she did not want Cindy to transition into a full-blown anxiety attack before entering the hospice center.

Cindy dropped her head onto her chest. She knew what she had to do, but it was not easy. She was always there for her mom and her mom was always there for her. What was going to happen now?

"Dr. Jeanine, will my mom ever get better? Can we give her more medicine? Can we send her somewhere where they can fix her? I keep hearing how so many people are cancer survivors. Can't my mom be one of them?"

Jeanine felt her chest tighten. *Oh, Cindy, she thought to herself. This is going to be the absolute hardest thing you will ever face in your lifetime. I wish I could make it easier for you, but, damn, cancer sucks.*

Jeanine realized she had to answer Cindy. She could not let Cindy go in and see her mom and believed her mom was going to pull through. She wasn't going to – not this time. And, in fact, Cindy was running out of time and needed to get inside. Now.

"Cindy," Jeanine expressed in her softest mom voice and not the official doctor tone, "Baby, you need to go and see your mom. This might be your…" Jeanine could not finish.

Cindy understood all too well. She unbuckled her seatbelt, opened the car door, and closed it gently. She turned to look at Jeanine and whispered, her words barely audible, "Thank you." And then she staggered up the brick-lined walkway and guardedly opened the door.

Cindy gazed back at Jeanine and Jeanine smiled and nodded before Cindy stepped over the threshold. Cindy had attempted to smile back, but her face felt frozen in place. She walked into the home and closed the door.

Riley sat up in the back seat. "What now, Mom? What do we do? We can't go in there, can we? What's going to happen? Are we going to sit here and wait till Cindy comes out? Does that mean her mom is going to die and then she will come out?

"I'm sorry, Mom, I know this sounds extremely callous and all, but, like, this is so new, and I'm incredibly sad for Cindy. I'm sorry for her because what's going to happen next for Cindy? Oh, jeez, I'm rambling." "

Jeanine put her hand on Gunther's shoulder for support and turned around to talk to Riley,

"Riley, my love, Cindy's mother is about to die. Her organs have shut down and the chemo was not working for her. The cancer has spread too far and I only hope she can open her eyes and see Cindy for one last time."

"But, Mom," demanded Riley, "If Cindy's mom dies today, where will Cindy go? She has no dad, no grandparents, no relatives that she knows of cause she told me so. She'll be an orphan and then what? Mom, what can we do?"

These were tough questions, but Jeanine had been thinking of them quite seriously for the last few months. She had been checking in on Mattie almost daily and was frustrated that the chemicals were not responding to her cancer. It wasn't fair. Cancer never was. It took the young, the old, the rich, the poor, no matter the race or religion. It left holes in people's hearts that could never be mended.

During the past few months, Mattie had confided in

Jeanine. She told her where she had left a will, where she wanted to be buried, and where her life insurance policy was kept. There wasn't much left over for Cindy, but enough to help her through the next few years, except… except…where would Cindy go and with whom?

Jeanine had offered to adopt Cindy, but Mattie was vehement about that. She felt it would be more of a burden since she already had Riley plus having two doctors as parents was stressful enough.

And then Mattie had an idea. She thought it was crazy, but she asked Jeanine if one of Cindy's teachers, a Mrs. Neva Waverly, could come visit her. She needed to talk with her. And Jeanine did just that. She called Mrs. Waverly, and she came to see Mattie right away. The two of them had a private conversation and Jeanine was not told what that conversation was about until yesterday. But it was not up to her to share that information with Cindy. Not yet, anyway.

• • •

The home was the biggest mansion Cindy had ever seen. The inside foyer was bigger than her entire living room. It was beautiful with wooden paneling and a humongous chandelier that sprinkled a multitude of colors throughout the pink-marbled floor.

A tall woman with a gray bun on top of her head and tiny jeweled glasses on her nose came into the foyer.

"Hello there, young lady. How can I help you?"

"Uhh, my mom…um…Mattie Newport. She's my mom. I was told to come see her today."

The woman reached both hands out to Cindy in a gesture that was not comfortable with Cindy. She did not know how to respond. The woman, who introduced herself as Ms. Clarke, took both of Cindy's hands in hers and squeezed them gently.

"Come, my dear. Let me take you to your mother. She is waiting to see you." And with that, she put her arm around Cindy and guided her down the hall.

There were numerous rooms along the hallway. Some of the doors were open and Cindy glanced in them as she walked by, her legs numb but somehow they kept moving. There were beds in each of the rooms and Cindy could see that each room was individualized with personal effects but none that she could identify. Her mind wasn't there to figure out these things; she kept up with Ms. Clarke and the walk seemed to take forever.

How much of a forever would Cindy have with her mom?

CHAPTER 20

Neva loved visiting her sister, Kathleen. They had always been close, and Kathleen knew all of Neva's skeletons from her failed marriage to her miscarriage to her crushed dreams of motherhood. Neva felt as though she never had to hide anything from Kathleen and that made their relationship very special.

Kathleen was also very open with Neva. She would tease Neva often with, "I'm named after our great grandmother, and you were just Neva-a-thought!"

"Oh," Neva would retort, "But mom couldn't come up with an original name so you were borrowed from the past which is why you just write about things that have already happened."

"Oh, ouch, that was a real low blow, my much older sister! And to think I invited you here because I love you."

"Hmmmmm, and I thought it was because you finally needed someone to teach you how to cook food that's truly edible!"

And so on and so on. The two of them teased each other and hugged and laughed so hard they would both cry till they fell over onto each other.

The two of them were sitting on Kathleen's patio facing the ocean. The sky was cerulean blue without a cloud anywhere in sight. The morning marine layer had finally dissipated and the gentle breeze flowing over them was as gentle as a kiss.

"I miss this part, Kathy," Neva said with a yearning in her heart. "I love the East Coast with the fall and winters and I truly love my job, but there is something about sitting here staring out into that gorgeous, mysterious ocean that makes me want to drop everything and move in with you."

"Urgggghhhh," spit Kathleen, her mouth filled with a California burrito she just had Door Dashed a few minutes ago. She swallowed her huge bite, the green salsa slowly dripping down her chin. Neva reached over with her napkin and lightly wiped it away.

"But, Neva, you needed to be near mom and dad, remember? If it wasn't for you, Sis, I wouldn't have had the opportunity to move out here and work on the magazine. You made that happen for me. You sacrificed for me. And I will never, ever let you forget that."

Neva nodded. "I did it because I love you and I wanted you to be able to chase your dream. My dream, well, the marriage and the baby part, was like a shooting star — it was bright and beautiful and then it shot up and exploded.

"I can't even think about what my life would have been like had things been different. Oh, well, they say things happen for a reason. And quite honestly, I love teaching; I love my students. They mean the world to me. Do you know I am still in touch with a few of them on social media? I love it. I love seeing where they have gone and what they have achieved with their lives. It makes me feel as though I had shared with them the tiniest bit of inspiration and positive vibes that helped them explode with their own visions."

Kathleen nodded, her green eyes, just a shade darker than Neva's, were glistening. She took another bite of her burrito and urged Neva to eat as well. "Neva, baby, you're getting too thin. Now eat this special California burrito because, honey, you ain't *neva* gonna find this anywhere east of here!"

Neva smiled. She leaned back and let the sun rest on her face. She would enjoy this moment a bit longer before she ate. Besides, she had something to share with Kathleen and she needed to build up a little more courage.

"So, what's in store for us today, Sis," Neva asked, her eyes still closed as she absorbed the California sun.

"Well, I already made dinner reservations at my favorite sushi place. You are gonna love it! The chef will keep creating sushi sensations for us until we cry stop!

"But, after you down that burrito that is still resting in front of you, we are going to go for a hike in the hills. I want to visit a friend of mine who has a passion fruit farm. She continues to beg me to grab a bushel to take home, and besides, I want you to meet her. I wrote an article about her last season."

"Passion fruit? I don't remember eating that last time. What's it like?"

"Ummmm, it's hard to describe. The outside looks like a delicious ruby red hard apple, and the inside honestly, well, it looks like mushy dark-green pomegranate seeds surrounded by golden yellow pulp. And then you scoop out all this goodness and place the heavenly fruit on ice cream or even an açai bowl, and it's positively fabulous. I met MaryFaith quite a few years ago at the local farmer's market and we became fast friends. She has over one hundred passion fruit vines along her deer fence."

"Wow. That's sound awesome. Uhhh, so what kind of article did you write? You usually send me copies of your stuff. What's up with that?"

Kathleen stopped chewing for a while. She put her burrito down and stared out into the ocean. "I didn't want to upset you, so I didn't send you a copy of it. I can show you later. Bottom line, MaryFaith owns the farm with her husband, and she was busy in the kitchen one night as she usually is when suddenly she heard some noise out in the back.

"Well, she stops cleaning the dishes, dries her hands on her towel, and strolls out back. She wasn't in a hurry, just curious. Just at that moment, she sees her little pup, Cooper, in the mouth of a coyote who was sprinting along the deer fence where there happened to be a hole in the fence."

Neva sat up, her mouth wide open and her eyes fixed on Kathleen. "NO! That coyote did not grab that poor little puppy and take off!" Neva was horrified.

"I'm sorry to tell you this, Neva. That's why I never sent you the article. I was writing about some of the horrors of living in the hills when the coyotes slink down and hunt not just for rabbits, but for any small mammals they can grab in their mouths. And that includes small dogs! I didn't want to upset you. I mean I know Atticus is a huge dog and all, but I knew this would upset you too much."

Neva let her head fall onto her chest, her dark frizzy hair falling into her face. "Oh, Kathy, that is so so sad."

"What made it worse," Kathleen continued, "was Mary-Faith blamed herself for not seeing the hole in the fence and forgetting she had let her pup out in the back. Now she never lets her other dog outside unless she is with him."

The two were silent for the next few minutes.

"Okay, Neva-Better, so it's time to catch me up on your school gossip. I need to hear to scoop. What's the word with your friend Carl and his girlfriend DD?"

Neva laughed. She needed that. She did not want to be in a depressed mood. "Hahahah, her name is CC, you goof! It's short for Cassandra Conway. And to tell you the truth I wouldn't doubt it if the two of them get married before we start the new school year. They are a match made in heaven if you ask me, and I love them both to death!"

"Oh, very nice! And on a darker note, what about that evil teacher you told me she might have stirred up some ugly rumor or something – Beverly? Is that her name?"

"Yeah, good memory. From what I heard, she confessed to a huge lie about Carl and then she had a major mental breakdown. Last I heard she was in some psych ward or something. I'm hoping she never comes back to teaching. Evil does not even come close to what kind of woman she is and what horrible heinous acts she is capable of committing."

"Wow. That school of yours is something else. Maybe I should write an article about the ins and outs of what actually happens in a schoolyard. Ain't nothing like the Paul Simon song, huh?"

Neva and Kathleen finished their burritos and gulped down their Modelo beers. They were quite satiated.

The two of them sat there soaking up the sun, the air, and their closeness.

Finally, Neva sat up. She took another swig of her Modelo for bravery, cleared her throat, and declared, "Uhhh, Sis, love of my life and protector of all our memories, I need to talk to you about something. Something that recently cropped up and, I need to share it with you and you alone, at least, for now. I need to know if you think I'm doing the right thing. I'm kinda nervous, super scared, and then again incredibly excited."

Kathleen opened her eyes and stared at Neva. She adored her older sister, and when Neva acted like this, well the last time was when Neva took off for Europe for several months and was off the grid. Kathleen was hoping this wasn't going to be this serious.

"Go on, Nev…tell me…just get it off your chest. I'm here for you, my darling sister. No matter what it is or how bad it is, I'm here for you."

"Oh, Kathy, it's not a negative thing. It's an incredibly beautiful thing. You see, well, one part of it is not beautiful."

"Okay," mumbled Kathleen, the cold beer slurring her words a bit, "you are making me crazy already. Spit it out, woman, and get to the point, or do I have to read the entire novel?"

Neva let out a nervous laugh, stumbled, and forged ahead. "You see, there is a student of mine. Her mother has triple-negative breast cancer…"

"Oh, Neva, that's awful. But it's treatable, right?"

"Well, yes, usually. But in this case, the mom wasn't able to respond positively to her chemotherapy treatments. And, sadly, the cancer has spread to other parts of her body. And, Kath, she's dying. I didn't realize how quickly she was declining but it's happened very fast. Too fast."

"Oh, no!" Kathleen stammered rubbing her arms vigorously as goosebumps spread on her arms and neck.

"On top of that, do you remember I had a good friend I met in college named William Tydings?"

"Hahaha, you mean Billy the Wolf?"

"God, you have such a memory! Yes, we were in a couple of early education classes at college. He was there because he was studying animal husbandry, but he only stayed for oh, maybe two years. He wanted to become a special education teacher, but he had to leave to take care of his farm after his parents both passed. So now he is running the horse farm, and would you believe in the summer he has a camp with designated horses for children with special needs?"

"Okay, where are you going with this? Are you and Billy the Wolf getting together? Are you getting married and you didn't tell me? Tell me, quick before I pass out from the beer!"

Neva smiled. "That's not a terrible thought, the marriage part, not you passing out, but no, it's nothing like that. I contacted him this past spring because I wanted to send one of my students there for the summer. As a counselor of course. She has a passion for horses and I thought this would be a wonderful experience for her. In addition," Neva paused here.

"Yes, Nev…in addition, what?"

Neva took a deep breath. "Her name is Cindy and it's her mother who is dying from this damn cancer. I thought if she were able to be away for the summer she might not have to deal with seeing her mother waste away in front of her eyes every day."

"Neva, that's very sweet and all. But, I can tell, there is more here. Go on."

"Yes, there is so much more. Patience, my adorable little sister. Before I left on vacation and, by the way, I left Atticus with Carl. Carl is great with Atticus, but CC adores him even more."

"You're hedging…stop it…tell me more about Cindy and her mother."

Neva nodded. "Yes, okay. Right before I left on my vacation, Cindy's mother, Mattie, called me and asked me to please visit with her. I had no clue why she would want to see me. I mean I think Cindy is a sweetheart and I have seen her grow so much this year…"

"Neva!"

"Yes, I'm getting to it. So naturally I went to see Cindy's mother."

"Her name? Did you tell me?"

"Hm, not sure. Her name is Mattie. It just so happened that when I went to see her it was her last day at the hospital. One of her doctors is the mom of another one of my students; her name is Riley. Anyway, Riley's mother, Dr. Jeanine Maddox, took me into her office at the hospital and told me that Mattie was not responding to her treatment and that she was being moved to hospice. She and her husband and Riley were going to get Cindy from the camp the next day and bring her to see her mother… before…" Neva choked and coughed until tears slipped from her eyes.

Kathleen reached over and squeezed Neva's hands. "It's okay, baby, I'm here with you. Tell me the rest."

Neva swallowed, rubbed her eyes, took another sip, and started over. "So I went to see Mattie; she was so weak. The poor thing had lost so much weight since I had met her on back-to-school night last year. She didn't look anything like the woman I had met before.

"Anyway, she could barely talk, but she had some papers in her hands. They looked legal or something. I don't know. I took her hand in mine. She smiled weakly. She looked up at me and said, 'Cindy adores you, Mrs. Waverly, and…" Mattie stopped and tried to catch her breath. She had labored breathing and could barely get the words out without stopping to rest.

"I don't have…much time," she continued haltingly, "Cindy…has no…family. I'm going to ask you…I need to ask you… I know…this is a…huge imposition…and you can say no…but…Mrs. Waverly, would you legally adopt my daughter and take care of her for me? I'm begging you. There is…enough money in my will…to help with…her cost…and all."

Neva stopped. She could not say another word. Her head fell onto her chest and the tears rolled down her cheeks as she sobbed uncontrollably.

Kathleen grabbed her sister and hugged her tightly.

"Oh, Neva, that's the most beautiful thing I have ever heard!"

"No," cried Neva. "The most beautiful thing in the world is that I told her mother yes!"

CHAPTER 21

Lucas was staring into Miss Anna's deep hazel eyes, her glasses pushed up on top of her head and the reflection in the glasses from the overhead lights splashed dots of multi-colored lights on the posters on the wall.

"So, Lucas," inquired Anna, "tell me about this last trip you had with your stepfather, Walter.

"You know," declared Lucas with a bit of annoyance in his voice, "I didn't want to go camping with him; I didn't want to do anything with him."

"Hmmmm, I see."

Lucas hated it when she said 'I see' because it meant he had to continue with his thought process and he wasn't in the mood. Julie, his mom, had dropped him off thirty minutes ago. It was too soon for his appointment but she had to run into CVS and pick up some meds.

Lucas had watched his mother drive off and for a split second, he eyed the road going the other way. He stared at the road, his chest heaving. His breathing was erratic and he wanted to punch something. Anything. He was tempted to just run as fast as he could for as long as he could just to avoid going in to see his therapist.

Lucas liked Miss Anna. He liked her from the very start even though he swore he was going to despise her like crazy, but she had won him over. She was sweet and kind and most important of all, she listened to him. She never made him feel stupid or crazy for his thoughts. She knew what his father had done to him, and she never tossed that back at him or used that as justification for his erratic and inappropriate behaviors.

But she did push him ever so tenderly and he relaxed with her and as his friends would say he eventually spilled his guts. He practically threw up all over her with his intense disgust for his father and added to that he could not – would not ever accept a stepfather let alone an African American stepfather. It was not something he could willingly accept. Not ever.

Lucas grunted and looked away from Miss Anna. He gazed at the various posters on the wall and then stopped short. His mouth dropped open for a second and then he clamped it shut almost like a robot malfunctioning. Sweat gathered on his forehead and his hands shook. He grasped them and squeezed them tightly willing the trembling to stop.

Anna's knowing eyes traveled from Lucas's easy gawking of her collections of posters to a beeline to the exact poster that initiated him to segue into anxiety mode. "See something over there?" Anna poked carefully but with a gentle force recognizing that he needed to unwrap the emotions that triggered this sudden panic attack.

Lucas's heart was pounding so forcibly in his chest that he was sure Anna could hear it. Anna leaned forward, her knees almost touching Lucas while her hands were clasped together on her lap. She whispered slowly and methodically, "Hey, Lucas, I'm right here. You are in my office and you are safe. Breathe for me, hon, breathe one, two, three. In and out. There you go. Easy. Slowly. That's it.

"It's just you and me here. No one else." Anna turned her head slightly over her shoulder to see again which poster had triggered his anxiety.

Anna smiled to herself. Lucas had been staring at one of her favorite posters. It was a poster that depicted an old cabin on top of a mountain surrounded by higher snow-capped mountains. Anna had taken that picture years ago on her way into the Appalachian Mountains and loved it so much that she had it enlarged as a poster. On days when she had concluded a tough session, she would stare at that cabin in the mountains and reflect on the happy and peaceful times she had when she had camped near there. It calmed her; it made her smile.

But right now she had to focus on Lucas and ease him into functioning at a level where he could articulate why that particular poster activated such an immediate response that threw him into an intense panic attack.

Five minutes crawled by. Then another ten sludged through like a snail on the wet sand and Anna stared silently as the second hand on her wall clock forced itself to move. It felt as if Lucas was not going to recover from this when finally she heard him breathing regularly again. Lucas gradually lifted his head from his chest and using his forearm wiped the collected beads of sweat from his forehead. Anna murmured softly, "Lucas, can you tell me what you were seeing up there on my wall?"

Lucas was focusing on his breathing and could not hear Anna. When he zoned out like this, surrounding voices sounded like he was under water. He knew Anna was saying something but he could not make out her words; the sounds were garbled and he was too focused on his breathing.

His chin sank back onto his chest. Why did this have to hurt so much he thought? Would the pain ever go away? When will I be normal again? Will I ever be myself? Ever?

Anna waited patiently. She needed Lucas to shift from his dull conscious state to being fully alert enough to deal with this last episode. She eyed her wristwatch subtly so as not to let Lucas see her checking the time. She was not worried about how much time had passed; no, she did not want to finish this session without him being able to reveal what triggered him to spiral so quickly.

"Lucas? Lucas?"

Lucas closed his eyes and shook his head, his soft curly brown hair falling into his eyes. He sat like that for just a moment, took a deep breath, and sat up. His right hand reached up to his forehead and pushed his hair back over his head and he looked straight at Anna.

Lucas knew he had to talk to his therapist. She had to hear everything because she was there for him and he needed her. He could not continue like this. He was physically and mentally exhausted and if that meant sharing all his pain and fears with someone who could help him then he needed to grow a set and move on. He was too old to sit in the corner, cry, and feel sorry for himself. It was time, and he recognized it. Finally.

"Miss Anna," he mumbled, "This past weekend, Walter and I…" Lucas stopped. His mother had been begging him not to call him Walter. She wanted Lucas to call him Dad. Afterall, Julie and Walter had been married for a few years now.

Anna saw Lucas's face twitch. Another trigger she thought to herself and let that piece of information marinate for a while.

"Go on, Lucas," Anna encouraged. "It's okay. What's in the poster that made you recall your weekend trip with him?" She purposely did not call him Walter and she knew it was too raw to refer to him as his father.

Lucas stammered at first, cleared his throat, and then spoke slowly and clearly, "The two of us were going on a fishing trip at the river for the weekend. Just him and me. The coach knew we were going away so I wouldn't get in trouble for missing football practice and well…"

Anna knew not to push. She saw Lucas struggling to continue and she empathized with his pain. She wished she could wave a magic wand over him and erase those heinous memories but the reality was he had to face it.

Lucas had to walk into that room packed with his fears and horrible memories and emerge cleansed and whole. And Anna was willing to be with him every step of the way.

"We were just driving along the highway, you know," Lucas continued speaking carefully and methodically.

"Damn, Miss Anna, and then it happened…again!" Lucas jumped up and balled both his hands and if she had a punching bag hanging from the ceiling he would have attacked it with all his might.

And then Lucas froze, looked straight at the guilty poster as if he were testing himself, relaxed his hands, and sat back down.

"But this time, jeez, this time it was different. I was sweating and shaking and feeling like I was falling into the deepest hole, free falling and going faster and faster and then…

"And then I felt Walter holding me. He was holding me tight. But it wasn't…it wasn't…" Lucas started choking, hot tears sluicing down his reddened cheeks. "It wasn't a bad hold, ya know, not like…not like before."

Lucas looked up at Anna, not embarrassed by his tears or the snot running from his swollen red nose, and cried, "I wanted to call him Dad, Miss Anna. I wanted him to hold me and tell me I was going to be okay. I didn't care that he was not my real dad. Hell, I'm never going to see my real dad ever again, but Walter, I never wanted to admit it; I never wanted to accept it."

Anna did not want to interrupt, but she slipped in with, "Admit what, Lucas?"

Lucas took a cleansing breath, and then another.

"I never wanted to admit that I like Walter. He's really good to me and especially to my mom. But if I call him dad, what does that do to my real dad? Are those memories ever going to disappear, Miss Anna? Ever?"

Anna hurt. Her chest tightened and tears threatened to roll down her face, but she forced herself not to display her emotions. It was not professional, but it hurt her so deeply to see her clients in pain. She had to believe that with time and more sessions with her, Lucas would heal those scars and allow himself to see a bright future. She had to believe that or she would never have taken the career path she had.

"Yes, Lucas," she sighed, "I promise you it is going to get better. Each day, each weekend, each holiday that you have good memories with Walter and your mom, it's going to be easier, and you know what else?"

Lucas snorted.

Anna took that as her cue to continue. "Your next step is to try, try to let the word 'dad' slip out of your mouth. It's not going to be easy at first. You might even feel like you're being fake or worse like you want to throw up or something."

Lucas smiled. Miss Anna could somehow see what he was thinking.

"Yes, Lucas," Anna declared in a strong tone, "I need you to try to call him dad before you come back for our next session. I won't ask you to count as to how many times you call him that, but you are going to say it at least one time. Promise me?"

Lucas groaned. "Do I really have to?"

Anna nodded. "Yes, you do because each time you say that word, it's going to start to feel normal again and then you won't even realize you're saying it. Like calling your football plays over and over again, only you won't need to write the word on your arm."

Lucas and Anna both laughed at that image. "Okay, Lucas. You go on and get out of here today and I look forward to seeing you next week. Take care. And, hey, give your mom a hug for bringing you here, okay?"

Lucas stood up, smiled, and raised his arm as the two of them did a quick fist punch and he exclaimed, "Peace out, Miss Anna. Till next week."

CHAPTER 22

The room was quiet. A soft pall seemed to float in the air as the four people sat deathly still and quiet. No one was making eye contact. No one was moving. No one was speaking and the soft sound of the air conditioning humming in the background lightly cracked the silence like a frozen lake splitting apart. Brynley and Berkley looked at each other, surreptitiously, nervously as to why Shaynee had asked them to get together with no one else in the room except Stetson.

The two women shifted in their seats. For a split second Berkley reached over to Brynley to take her hand like they used to when they were young and were being scolded by their parents, and then she quickly pulled her hand back and let it rest in her lap.

Shaynee and Stetson stared at their mothers, eyeing them as if for the very first time. To get this special meeting alone without the boys and Bryant was something of a miracle and Shaynee knew she was on limited time. The clock was ticking almost as loud and fast as her heart.

Shaynee thought back to when she and Stetson had met at Starbucks. Was it only last week that Shaynee had ripped apart Stetson's world at Starbucks with the shocking news? She had stared at her cousin/twin, Stetson, drinking his second frappe without a care in the world. The revelation had hit her like a cold slap in the face.

She studied Stetson. Why had it taken so long for her to see the obvious? Shaynee looked around her making sure no one was close enough to hear her speak. It was bad enough Riley had opened her mouth and dropped the bomb before she had the chance to work her magic with Stetson. Stetson always listened to Shaynee, followed her advice, and pretty much did whatever Shaynee told him to do. Whether it was telling him which girls to avoid, what to study for in their classes, or even what the answers were on the tests that Shaynee had already taken the day before. Legit or not, Stetson was her blood and she would do whatever she needed to in order to help him along his pathways.

Shaynee turned around to see Mrs. Truglio with her husband sipping their chai lattes with their local papers in their hands. They lived down the street from Shaynee and were always so nice to her. For Christmas, Mrs. Truglio baked special Italian cookies and gave her and her twin brothers, Colton and Cameron, a box of her special treats.

"It's okay, Mrs. Truglio," said Shaynee. "I'm just messing with my cousin. You know him, it's Stetson."

Mrs. Truglio shook her frail head up and down, her thinning white hair shining in the overhead lights. "Okay, I just didn't know if I had to call on Ilene over there. You know the sweet lady who makes my tea every day? She looks out for my Rolan and me. And…"

Shaynee hated to be rude, but she was losing ground with Stetson who had already pulled his phone back out of his pocket and was busy scrolling. "Thanks again, Mrs. Truglio." And with that, Shaynee turned back to scowl at Stetson who immediately cleared his throat and slid his phone back into his pocket.

It was only after this that Shaynee had finally explained everything to Stetson, and showed him his DNA results and their connection to a total stranger. Stetson had not handled all the information very well since he ended up vomiting outside the store. It was not Shaynee's favorite memory, but she had told Stetson everything. And when they were sitting on the bench that day, she told him that together they needed to find out the truth from their moms. Who was their real, no that's not the correct wording, thought Shaynee, it was who was their biological mom? Shaynee made their moms come to this meeting without the boys and Bryant. And so, Shaynee knew she had to move things along or they would never find out the truth.

They were sitting in the living room with her mom and her Aunt Brynley, Stetson's mom. How to begin? Where to start? How was Shaynee going to explain this? How could she even begin to ask the hard questions?

Finally, Berkley looked at her daughter and Stetson and then her own sister. "Shaynee, hon, why have you asked us here? You specifically said for Dad to take the boys to the mall because you had something you needed to discuss with only us. So, here we are, but no one is talking. You and Stetson keep staring at each other like you have a deep dark secret that is about to explode so unless you want me to stick one of you with a pin, give it up! And now!"

Shaynee adjusted herself on the couch and Stetson coughed and cleared his throat.

At the exact same time, both of them started to speak and then they looked at each other and laughed uncomfortably. This was not going to be easy. How much longer could Shaynee stall them? How much more of a conversation could they have before her father burst into the room and completely ruined what Shaynee had planned?

Shaynee struggled to control her emotions and she felt that if something didn't happen in just a few seconds, her entire secret operation was going to blow up in her face. She stood up and nervously waved her hands.

"Mom," she began slowly. "Aunt Bryn, it's like this. Uh-hhh, Stetson and I have been talking and getting together and…"

Now Brynley stood up, her anxiety over all of this secretiveness unnerving her, "Shay, baby, what exactly are you trying to say? Is something wrong? Did Stetson get in trouble and you're both trying to let us know in some way?"

It was Stetson's turn to react. He stood up, his pouting lips wet with anger, "Why is it always me who is in trouble?

You know, Shaynee has her own issues if you must know and I'm not about to get into that cause that's on her, and if she hadn't made me do that thing for her we wouldn't even be here right now and I would be with my friends doing whatever…"

Brynley's eyes widened and her mouth opened and she gasped, "What do you mean 'that thing for her'? What are you talking about? Was Shaynee in trouble?"

Berkley jumped up and grabbed Brynley. "Now listen, Sis, it can't be Shaynee who's in trouble because," Berkley stopped abruptly and turned to Shaynee and whispered, "Are you? Is it you? Did you have…"

Shaynee held up her hands. "Okay, everybody, stop. I mean STOP right now! Let's all sit down and start this over. I mean it!" Shaynee's eyes burned with anger and she stared hard at everyone including Stetson.

Shaynee walked over to Brynley and Berkley. She held back tears, her shoulders sagging as she reached for a hand from each of the women who sat rocking back and forth on the couch, nervous energy combined with a fear of the unknown.

Shaynee, gaining a newfound strength in her convictions, declared, "You know Stetson and I will be filing for our driver's permit next month. I guess you know what that means, right? Like we will need to see our birth certificates. You do have our birth certificates, huh?"

Berkley gasped. Brynley's head dropped onto her chest.

Berkley stuttered, "Uh, baby, you know I am not exactly

sure where that is. Hmm, Bryn, do you have Stetson's birth certificate?"

Brynley burped loudly. She had a rare reaction to nerves and whenever she was upset, she burped – loud and uncontrollably. And she was doing it over and over. Shaynee always thought it was seriously gross, but that was her aunt.

Berkley leaned over and squeezed her sister's shoulders. "It's okay, love. Maybe, just maybe, it's time, you know? Maybe this is the time we share…"

Shaynee swallowed hard. She did not like the way her mom and her Aunt Brynley were acting. They looked uncomfortable, uneasy. This was not going to be as simple as she had anticipated. Shaynee thought there would be cheering and clapping and congratulations and high-fives everywhere. But now she was having second thoughts about all of it. Especially about secretly reaching out to a stranger last week. Reaching out to someone she did not know or let anyone else know what she had done.

Shaynee's hands turned clammy and she looked over her shoulder to Stetson who was staring at his mother, his head cocked to one side, confused at the way the women were acting. He looked at Shaynee and his eyes said it all. They had never acted so…how could Stetson describe it? Weird? Scared? Ashamed? All of the above. Stetson turned his head to look at the two women he loved with all his heart and then back again to Shaynee. This was all happening too fast.

Shaynee glared at Stetson, held up her arms, and gave

him that look that said, Oh, no! We opened up a can of worms that can never be closed ever again.

Just then the doorbell rang and everyone froze. The four family members stared at each other as though a bomb had just dropped on their house.

Shaynee responded first. "I'll get the door!" And she ran to the front door. The rest of the group stood up in silence each with their own dark thoughts about what was happening.

Suddenly, Shaynee strolled into the living room, her hand grasping tightly onto a man's hand.

"Mom, Aunt Brynley, you might know this person, but Stetson, I want you to meet Ronnie Torres, our father."

CHAPTER 23

Cindy hated hospitals. The antiseptic smell made her gag, the long hallways gave her anxiety, and the overhead lights made her dizzy. But this building was not a hospital. Dr. Maddox had told her so softly Cindy wasn't sure she had heard her. Dr. Maddox explained that this was hospice. Hospice? That sounded like a hospital, but she gathered it wasn't. It just looked like a huge house from the outside.

Before Cindy had opened the door she looked back for Riley. But Riley was smothered in a tight hug by both her parents. Riley never cried and this huge show of emotion unnerved her, but she did not have time to process what was happening as the woman named Ms. Clarke was escorting her to mom's room.

There were so many rooms they began to blur together. Ms. Clarke was talking but Cindy was in another zone. She heard a voice, but it seemed as though it was far off and indistinguishable.

Ms. Clarke turned a corner and suddenly they were in a small kitchen. A woman was sitting by herself by the table. She was moaning and her small hands were pressed on her forehead. Her stringy gray hair hung limply around her face.

Ms. Clarke halted in front of her and Cindy almost plowed into her. Ms. Clarke gently placed her hands on the woman's shoulders and murmured, "Hello, Mrs. Hermine. How are you feeling today."

Mrs. Hermine looked up, her silver glassy eyes wet with tears. "Where are they? Why aren't they coming? They were supposed to be here."

Ms. Clarke nodded and with compassionate tones whispered, "It's okay, Mrs. Hermine. I'll check to see where they are, okay? You just stay put here for a little while and I will come back. Would you like some of that nice Jello you love?"

Mrs. Hermine nodded and sobbed at the same time. Cindy was confused. Was this a hospital? Was this some kind of rehab that she heard about in her health class? The woman didn't look sick, but she didn't look so great either.

"Here's your Jello, hon, and you enjoy it. I'm taking Miss Cindy here to see her mom and then I will be right back to see you. Okay?" Mrs. Hermine smiled weakly and dug her spoon into her cup of Jello. The red jiggly stuff did not make it up to her mouth on the spoon and as Cindy was following Ms. Clarke out of the kitchen, she noticed the woman scooping up the bits of Jello with her long fingers.

"C'mon, Miss Cindy. Your mom is just around the corner here."

Cindy stayed close to this woman who seemed to be in charge of this house and Cindy was already confused about where she was in the house. For a quick moment, she feared losing herself and never finding her way out.

The two of them waltzed through another room. To Cindy, it looked like a family room. There was a large television on the wall surrounded by a couple of bookcases that were filled with various books. A large comfortable couch was opposite the television. An elderly man sat on the corner of the couch. Cindy could see his large gnarled hands curled tightly on a wooden cane. The bald man's head was resting on his chest and she could hear him snoring as they walked by.

Next to the couch, a woman sat in her wheelchair. She was staring at the television, but Cindy could not hear any sound coming from there. She could see some program, maybe it was a kind of nature show with animals and what appeared to be a veterinarian working on a small bird. Cindy looked away when the woman turned to look at her, but the woman did not say anything. Ms. Clarke did not want to stay here and she said quietly, "Enjoy your show, Mrs. Toppak. I will see you later for your dinner."

And so Cindy continued to follow Ms. Clarke. How much longer till she would see her mother? This was beginning to feel unnatural. Was her mother actually here? What was going on?

They walked quickly beyond the television room down another hallway that housed more bedrooms. Every room seemed to be filled with personal effects. How many people live here? Was this like a hotel? Cindy was going to ask Dr. Maddox more questions when she left here.

And there it was, the last room on the left. Ms. Clarke stopped, turned around, and took Cindy's hands in hers. "Now, Cindy, dear, your mother is very weak. She may not be able to talk very long with you. She wants to see you and even if she doesn't talk much, just you being here will make all the difference in the world to her. Are you ready to see her?"

Cindy felt her body temperature drop. She was cold. She was shivering and grabbed her hands together to help stop herself from shaking. She looked up at Ms. Clarke and nodded. "I'm ready. Please, let me see her now."

Ms. Clarke opened the door slowly and backed away. She raised her hand and motioned for Cindy to step inside. As soon as Cindy walked in, Ms. Clarke gently closed the door and left Cindy to be with Mattie alone.

Cindy stood completely still. Her body was paralyzed and she could not move her feet to go any closer to her mother's bed. Who was that woman lying so still on the bed in front of her? Cindy scanned the room and her eyes fell onto the pictures on the nightstand next to the bed. It was filled with framed pictures of Cindy and Mattie, Cindy alone, Cindy as a baby, and more recently in high school.

Cindy swallowed hard. She kept thinking about what Miss Anna had said to her in one of their early sessions – *Cindy, you are smarter than you think, stronger than you feel, and braver than you realize.* Oh, where was Miss Anna now? Please, Miss Anna, help me go see my mom. She is there right in front of me but I can't move. I can't breathe, oh dear God, I think I'm going to pass out.

And then out of nowhere, Cindy heard her mother. It was so soft, Cindy wasn't sure if it really was her mother talking or just Cindy wishing she could hear her.

Mattie mumbled, "Cin, my baby, is that you? Oh, my love, please come closer. I want to see you. Please."

Cindy took a deep breath and counted to herself, one, two, three…one…two…three.

"Y…y…yes, Mom, " Cindy stuttered, "It's me, Mommy. I'm here. I'm here for you."

Cindy shuffled slowly over to the bed. And there was Mattie. So pale, so thin, Cindy barely recognized her mother.

"Oh, Mommy. I love you so much. I have missed you so much." Cindy reached over to hug her mother and without any hesitation, she crawled into the bed with her. She touched her mother's cheek, which was hot and dry. Her face, always so beautiful, was emaciated.

Cindy reached over to Mattie's forehead and tenderly stroked it, pushing her soft dark hair back off her face. Cindy looked into Mattie's once clear crystal blue eyes that now seemed dull, surrounded by a pale yellow tinge.

Cindy leaned over to her mom and pressed her face against her mother. "Mommy, I love you. Please come home with me. I will take care of you. I promise. I will always be there for you. Please, please come home." Cindy tried to hold back the tears but it was no use, they were raining down her cheeks onto her neck creating goose bumps down her arms.

Mattie took her two arms, thin and bruised from injections, and cradled her baby girl. "Oh, my baby. I love you with all of my heart." Mattie had to stop talking and take a breath. She was weak and could barely move.

"Cindy," Mattie stammered, "Cin, listen to me. I am not going to be here for you, but…I…"

"Mom," Cindy interrupted, "please don't talk. Don't say things like that to me. I need you, Mommy. I can't be without you. You are all I have. All I want. Please, don't leave me. You can't."

"Cindy, I know you are…" Mattie stopped to catch her breath… "Strong. You…are…the best thing…in my life… but I am so sorry I can't stay with…you…"

"NO! Don't talk like that. Dr. Maddox will take you home and she'll help me take care of you. It will be okay. I will be there with you…always."

"No, baby, I…won't…I…can't…now listen to me…I have taken care of everything…for you…"

"STOP! I won't listen. I won't!"

Mattie closed her eyes. She could feel the room spinning. Her body was shutting down and she knew she only had a few more precious moments. She had to let her daughter know. She had to tell her who was going to take care of her. She would never leave her alone, ever. Damn it all, why did she have to go and get sick?

Cindy squeezed tightly against her mother, her body willing her to be healthy, to be okay, to stay with her. Cindy breathed in her mother's scent, the soft faded smell of lavender more of a memory than a present scent, but Cindy held on praying with her every being that her mother would make a miraculous turn around.

Mattie, getting weaker by the moment, took Cindy by the shoulders, and with the last of her human strength she whispered, "I asked your English teacher, Mrs. Waverly, to take care of you. And Cindy, she promised me she would. She thinks you are the sweetest, best girl in the world. And, Cindy, she laughed with me and then we cried together. Cindy, she is going to be there because my love, I will not. I'm so sorry I have to leave you. I am so…"

And Mattie closed her eyes, too weak to continue.

Cindy stared at her mother and hugged her until she felt Mattie's life escape.

Cindy opened her eyes wide and saw one small tear slide down from her mother's closed eye.

Cindy gasped. She leaned over and kissed her mother on her cheek feeling the lone warm tear on her lips. "Oh, Mommy. I love you so much. I will miss you every day of my life. I promise you that I will make you proud of me. I…promise." Cindy, sobbing onto her mother's neck, lay there, her arms gently cradling the lifeless body.

Cindy could not remember how long she lay there pressed against her mother, and she did not know when the room lost the daylight that had filtered like a prism of colors into the room. She did not remember Gunther

Maddox coming in, unfurling her from her mother's stiffening body, scooping her up so lightly, and carrying her out to their car. She did not remember being driven to the Maddox house where she was carried up to the guest room and laid to sleep under the covers.

She only remembered her vivid dreams of laughing and playing with her mother, going to the lake and having a picnic, and dancing in their living room to the music of her mother's favorite old goodies. It was a beautiful dream and Cindy did not want to wake up. She wanted to stay in her dream forever.

But forever only happens in fairy tales.

CHAPTER 24

The day was not going well for Lila. First, she had to deal with her son and his possibly pregnant girlfriend who was currently in a bed at the emergency room. That was an experience she was hoping she would never have – at least not with her son.

Lila had driven as fast as she could to the hospital. Every red light seemed to take forever and traffic seemed unusually heavy. Why aren't these people at work, Lila muttered to herself as she missed another light because she was so far behind the line of traffic.

Finally, reaching the hospital Lila parked her car and walked as briskly as she could in her high heels. She spotted Benjamin immediately standing shoulder to shoulder with her husband Darrius in the doorway of the emergency room. Benjamin was staring into space, his hands fidgetingg and his body shifting back and forth. As soon as Lila entered the sliding glass doors, Ben rushed over to them.

"Mom...oh thank God you are here. Dad is here with me and...Meadow...Meadow is..." Benjamin could not finish his sentence. His light hazel eyes were filled with tears and Lila felt her heart break in two at the sight of him.

"C'mere, my precious. Let me hold you for a minute." Lila pulled her son towards him and cradled his soft hair against her shoulder. Benjamin was already several inches taller than she was, and seeing how her husband was well over six feet, she knew Benjy was still growing. But holding him in her arms, she immediately transitioned into mommy mode and he was her little Benjy.

Ben's broad shoulders relaxed against Lila's embrace and tears poured down his flushed face, a broken dam he had stoically tried to control.

Darrius, however, was not so sympathetic to his oldest son. He put his large hand on his son's shaking shoulder, grasped it firmly, and demanded unpleasantly, "What the hell were you thinking, son? What was going on here that you and I have not had a conversation about only a few months ago?"

Ben pulled himself apart from his mother. Lila was not happy that Darrius was going to share their laundry out here in the lobby of the emergency room.

"Darrius, really! Now?? Can't this wait until we have some privacy at least? We are standing in the middle of the hospital lobby for Christ's sake. And, oh, no, dear God. Benjy, baby, turn around. Are these Meadow's parents rushing up the sidewalk right now?"

Ben turned around and his mouth dropped open.

"Mom! Dad! Shit…what do I say to them? Uhhh, can you help me, please?"

Darrius raised one eyebrow, his brown eyes dull with anger as he stated in the sternest clipped voice he could muster in this setting, "Son, you put yourself in this situation. An adult situation I might add. And now it's time for you to pull up your big boy pants and face the music. Turn around and walk up to her parents now and escort them in here to see their daughter immediately. Your mother and I will be sitting out here in the waiting room and respectfully will not interfere. You come and get us when it's time. And, yes, we will continue this conversation in the privacy of our home at a later time."

Meadow's parents, Lee and Rhona Solomon, rushed over to Ben, grabbed him by his arm, and immediately started asking questions. "Where is she, Ben? Is she hurt? Did you have a car accident? What happened? Can we see her? Ben could not distinguish which parent was plying him with questions; he felt like he was attacked by both of them at the same time.

Rhona suddenly turned around and her eyes opened wide as she assumed the two adults standing a few feet away were related to Ben.

Lila took this opportunity to step forward, her arm extended to shake hands when Rhona rushed over and hugged Lila so tightly, that Lila lost her breath for a moment. The smell of Shalimar perfume overtook Lila and she was about to gag when Lee invaded their space and grabbed Darrius by his arm, shaking it vigorously.

Lila and Darrius, together smiled and stumbled over the introductions, looked at Benjamin, and asked, "Well, young man, are you or are you not going to introduce us to Meadow's parents?"

Benjamin's soft caramel-toned skin was marked with two red blotches of embarrassment as the awkward greeting enveloped him like a cold wet rag.

"Oh, I'm s…sorry. Mom, Dad, I would like to introduce you to Mr. and Mrs. Solomon, Meadow's mom and dad."

Lila laughed at her son. With all his maturity, there were times like these that reminded her that her son was just sixteen years old and still uncomfortable in social graces.

"How do you do?" said Lila stepping forward and extending her arm again. "I'm Lila and this is my husband Darrius."

Darrius cleared his throat stepped forward, and the four adults stood closely together, a strange tenseness among them.

Lila responded quickly. "Please, Mrs. Solomon, you and your husband must go see Meadow now. We will wait until we hear from one of you or Benjy."

Rhona smiled weakly. "Thank you, and please, we are Rhona and Lee." She turned to her husband, grabbed his hand, and looked at Ben. "Ben, please take us to see Meadow now."

Lila and Darrius sat in the waiting room for over an hour before Ben appeared. They stood up and rushed over to him anxious to hear any news.

Ben was nervous, contrite, and scared all at once. He

looked at Lila and then at Darrius and started to speak, but he choked and sobbed.

Before Lila could move towards her son, Darrius grabbed him by his shoulders and pulled him into a hug only a dad could deliver and he said, his voice hoarse, "Just say it, Son. Whatever it is we will deal with it, but we need to know. Is Meadow alright?"

Ben stepped back from his father and looked at both his parents and half sobbing, half gasping cried, "She had… she…had…oh, God…she had a miscarriage. She's going to be alright, but, Mom, Dad, I swear, I didn't know she was pregnant until this morning when she was so sick and she was throwing up and almost fainting and…I…I s… sw…swear I didn't know…I…"

Lila looked at Benjamin and then at Darrius. She said in her strong principal-listen-to-me-now voice, "Go and say your goodbyes to Meadow and her parents. Meadow needs to be with them right now. We are going home. We will reserve all of our discussions with you when we are in the privacy of our home. Now go, Benjamin. Now."

Lila turned to Darrius and said, "You take him home. I need to go back to the office for a little while. You will wait until I return home before you have any discussions with that boy. Do I make myself clear?"

Darrius knew that tone. It did not happen often, but when it did, he respected it and backed off. He kissed Lila on the cheek and said softly, "Crystal clear, my love. See you when you get home."

And with that, her two men trudged out of the hospital,

the father gripping his son's shoulder, supporting him emotionally and physically. Lila stood there wishing she was anywhere else but here.

Back in her car, Lila drove a bit more relaxed and not hurried. She knew whatever was waiting for her back at school could wait. At least she hoped it could wait. One emergency a day was more than enough.

Lila sauntered the building, embracing the familiarity of "her house" as she called it in private. She breathed in the clean antiseptic scent of the newly washed floors and smiled. She made a mental note to compliment and thank her custodial team. They worked very hard over the summer and she was very appreciative. The summer days flew by too quickly, but Lila always enjoyed the slower pace of the building with repairs being done, classrooms being cleaned, and boxes of new materials and books and supplies being delivered daily. It energized her every summer and she looked forward to these days.

Once inside her office, Lila breathed in the quiet. For a moment it was as though what had just transpired was a dream, no, more like a nightmare. These were the occurrences she dealt with almost daily as a principal, not as a parent. How could this have happened she asked herself silently. She and Darrius were always open and honest with their children, especially when it came to issues such as sex, race, and religion. The topics of concern went on and on. There were no forbidden subject matters in her household. None. Her children knew they were biracial from an early age; they knew there would be prejudice against them in their lives and family conversations usually centered around how to respond to these varying degrees of acceptance or hatred.

Dinner conversations concentrated around everyone's daily activities and more often than not there was a question that Ben or Bessie would raise regarding something that took place that day.

Bessie would ask, "Mom, am I mostly Black or mostly white? Which box do I check on the questionnaire on the test?"

Ben was more concerned with, "Dad, do I go to a Black college or does it matter? Would the other kids think I was too white to be at…uh…what do they call them HPUC?"

Lila could not help but stifle a laugh. "Benjamin, I have told you this before, it is HBCU and it stands for Historically Black Colleges and Universities. Son, when you are ready to go on a college tour next summer, we will explore all our options. Now stop pushing your broccoli to the side of your plate and finish eating. And by the way, dishes are yours tonight since you failed to follow the chore chart this week!"

These family discussions were filled with laughter, anger, questions, and concerns and Lila loved every minute of it. But where did she and Darrius go wrong she wondered? How could her son have been so careless to have managed to impregnate his girlfriend? She knew her husband had numerous talks with Ben about sex and contraceptives. Were teenage boys so reckless that all common sense left them in the heat of the moment? She smiled recanting the mantra she had always told Ben – when the little head tells the big head what to do then you are in big trouble.

Lila sat at her desk reliving the events of the hospital and hoping that Meadow would recover quickly and be able to deal with the circumstances in the following days, and months. She thought about letting her parents know about Miss Anna in case they wanted their daughter to see a therapist. Oh, well, Lila pushed that out of her mind right now knowing she had to deal with the emails that seemed to be screaming at her begging for her attention.

Lila had just started answering the overwhelming number of emails on her computer when Jeff and Gloria crashed her peace into shards of broken glass. Amelia Goddard, Lila's most trustworthy secretary, had left the building to buy lunch for everyone in the office when Jeff Stineman and Gloria Lomack somehow slipped through the main office without attracting the attention of any of the other secretaries.

The two burst into Lila's office without knocking or announcing themselves.

"Dr. L.," began Gloria tersely, "I was just informed that Cindy Newport's mother has passed away. Breast cancer. She couldn't beat it."

Lila exhaled slowly. That woman never made a gentle entrance; Lila liked to joke to herself (and yes, it was mean), that Gloria blew in like she was speeding off the Belt Parkway in New York. Not only was her brusque entrance irritating, but Gloria was not the most compassionate counselor she had known. She dispersed great news, good news, and sad news with the same heavy hand all the time. Gloria only knew one speed, one tone, and one direction. It was exhausting to be in the same room with her.

"Yes, Gloria. Thank you for informing me. I will follow up. I am so sorry to hear this. Is this the young lady who Neva found the summer camp job up in the mountains? Poor thing. Her mother, you said, had breast cancer? Wait a second. I'm looking up more information."

Lila swiveled her chair over to her computer and after a few clicks was busy reading Cindy's file. "Oh, my," reported Lila, as she was busy combing through the notes on the computer. "She has no living relatives, no one. Hmmmm, I think this means we need to contact social services and our PPW. The pupil personnel worker is new to our building this year, so Gloria, I am going to need you to contact LuAnn as soon as possible. Explain all the details to her, and Gloria, take your time with LuAnn. This is her first year in this position and you don't want to overwhelm her before she even begins her first day."

Lila pushed away from the computer and since she felt she had finished with Gloria, turned her attention to Jeff.

"And, Jeff, by the way, how are you feeling today?"

Jeff Stineman shuffled his feet back and forth. "Uhh, well, Gloria and I have been talking and I decided…"

Gloria abruptly interrupted, "WE decided, Jeff. We did it together, remember? Jeez and hold the cream cheese… men!"

Jeff coughed and continued, "Yes, WE agreed that together we are going on a weight program. Something like

Weight Watchers or Overeaters Anonymous. Something…
uhh, we are still researching cause Gloria thinks we can get
a discount if we join together. Right?" He smiled weakly
and looked at Gloria, but her burning eyes left a scorching
mark on his chin and he quickly scanned the carpet for
salvation his double chin shaking from fear of any further
admonishment.

Lila needed to end this conversation instantly before
the two of them ended up on the floor wrestling each
other. "Thank you both. I will take it from here, oh, and
Gloria…and Jeff, should you want to attend any of Cindy's
mother's memorial, I will share any information I receive."
And with that, Lila turned to her computer with a tacit
understanding that the meeting was indeed concluded.

Gloria grabbed Jeff's arm and guided him out as quickly
as the two of them could march out of Lila's office.

CHAPTER 25

Neva was sitting by herself in the front row of the church. On the pew on the other side were Carl's brother Chip, his father Harry, little Emma, and Cassandra's mother and father. The program listed them as Isabel and Stanley Conway.

The wedding ceremony was short but beautiful. Cassandra wore a pale blue sleeveless chiffon dress with pearl earrings and a pearl necklace. She wore her long auburn hair side-swept-up with pearl barrettes. Emma, who loved CC with all her heart, asked if she could wear her hair in the exact same style as Cassandra along with a pale blue puffy dress. Emma was holding Cassandra's beautiful round bouquet overflowing with pink and white roses, a few blue Delphiniums, wax flowers, and a white hypericum held together with a white satin ribbon.

Seated behind Neva were a few friends of Carl's from his college years and while they may have looked a bit hung over from celebrating with Carl the night before, they were surprisingly quiet. Neva figured they were trying desperately not to throw up in the pews and upset everyone in the church.

Neva beamed. She was immensely happy for Carl, and of course, Cassandra, but her heart melted for Carl. He had been through so much and to see him this happy, Neva could not help but cry, soft happy tears. She had returned home from visiting her sister in California to a conflicting combination of tremendous joy and devastating sadness.

First, she was notified by a lawyer's office that Cindy's mother requested a meeting with her. When Neva arrived at the hospice center, she sat with Mattie for a long time. Mattie's cancer had all but consumed her. She did not look like the woman Neva had met with at the end of the school year when she had asked Mattie permission to take Cindy to the summer camp that a good friend of hers ran. Neva shared with Mattie how she had a good friend named Bill Tydings who owned a horse farm and during the summer months he organized a camp for kids with special needs. Neva wanted Cindy to work as a junior counselor at the camp.

Although Mattie could barely talk, she nodded her head and grasped Neva's hand shaking it up and down thanking her with her eyes. Neva smiled and promised that Cindy would be in good hands that summer and that Mattie would not have to worry about Cindy. This way Mattie could relax and hopefully let the meds help her.

But now, Neva was with Mattie and a lawyer who had written up numerous documents that the three of them were reading together. It was heartbreaking for Neva and she did her best to hold back her tears, but in the end, she and Mattie held onto each other and cried. Neva agreed to legally take on the role of Cindy's guardian per Mattie's dying wish. Neva was overwhelmed and honored.

That meeting was a few days ago. Neva put that information back in her mind and concentrated on the wedding ceremony today. She was ecstatic to be a part of this wonderful moment celebrating everything Carl and Cassandra. Tomorrow, she knew, would be a different story. Tomorrow she would attend Mattie Newport's funeral,

She sat up straight as Carl declared his vows. She listened intently because he had practiced the vows with Neva just last night and like a proud mom she leaned forward just a bit to make sure he did not miss a beat.

Carl spoke just above a whisper: "Ahh, my love. The moment I stared into your deep brown pools of joy I knew happiness. You have become my friend, my lover, my confidant, and my teacher. I promise to always respect you, love you with all my heart, do the dishes now and then, and share my dreams with you. Together let us grow old and hold one another when we cannot stand alone, pray for each other when our minds cannot, and see for one another when our eyes grow dim. Cassandra, I love you with all my heart today, tomorrow, and forever. I ask you to be my wife, to walk alongside me so that we may take this journey together and embrace all there is in the world for us."

Cassandra, her eyes wet with tears of joy and filled with

a love for Carl so intensely, she took a deep breath and blew it out slowly. "Carl, my love, ever since you leaned on my desk that day at work I fell hopelessly in love with you. You are the sweetest, most gentle man I know. When I listen to you read bedtime stories to Emma you make my heart melt. I pray that together we have a life filled with joy and health and lots and lots of crazy adventures. I will always be by your side; I believe in you; I believe in the magic you envelop your students in every day; I believe in the love you have for imparting knowledge and if I can I will be there when you need my help, my guidance, and my cooking. And if I could quote my favorite author, Elizabeth Barrett Browning when she wrote in Sonnet 43: 'I love thee to the depth and breadth and height/My soul can reach…I love thee to the level of every day's/Most quiet need/…—and, if God choose,/I shall but love thee better after death.'"

There was not a dry eye in that church that day, and afterward, the party that Cassandra's parents held for everyone was simple but elegant – just like the wedding ceremony.

Neva stayed for a little while, but needed to go home and start preparing for a life she had always longed for since she was young. She was going to formally adopt Cindy Newport and Neva could not be more excited than if she was getting married that day alongside Carl and Cassandra!

Nothing was going to spoil that day. And fortunately for Neva and more importantly, for Carl and Cassandra, no one in the church saw a car parked at the back of the lot under a tree hidden from view. No one would have paid any attention to a small car sitting innocuously in the shadows. No one unless they would have casually observed a woman with very short black hair and beady dark eyes hunched over the steering wheel staring into binoculars that were fixed on the church. No one would have ever believed evil would be parked so close to a church filled with love.

CHAPTER 26

They stood in a line shoulder to shoulder. They were all holding hands just like the football captains do when they march to the center of the field and meet the other team.

Jilly, Riley, Lucas, Junay, Aiden, Roland, Jáquan, Shaynee, Stetson, Sofia, Lane, Max, and Tommy with Cindy in the middle of the pack. They were there for her; they were her team and together they escorted her as she staggered towards the casket.

Behind them were many of Cindy's teachers from Wells High School including Principal Libertino, Assistant Principals Barbara Atkinson and Jeff Stineman, and Counselor Gloria Lomack. Miss Anna, her therapist, was there. Riley's parents, Drs. Jeanine and Gunther Maddox stood with Neva Waverly, Carl, and Cassandra. Following the group came Bill Tydings, the owner of the summer camp that Cindy had worked in during the summer.

The funeral was not long. The pastor spoke briefly. He

was a tall man with a head full of black hair and deep blue eyes that looked right into your soul. At least that was how Neva always felt when she attended church. He did not know Cindy or her mother, but Neva knew Pastor Craig for many years, and she shared with him everything she knew about Mattie and Cindy.

Pastor Craig stood there in front of Mattie's casket, both hands holding his bible in front of him. His head gazed upon the line of teenagers in front of him, stopping for a moment to smile at Cindy, and then he continued to make eye contact with the rest of the group. He swallowed slowly, cleared his throat, and then he began.

"Good morning, everyone. Cindy," and now he turned his head back to Cindy. "This morning we are gathered here to help you celebrate the life of your mother, Muriel Newport. While Mattie, as we called her, lived for only a short time on this earth, she made sure that each day she and her daughter, Cindy, experienced love and joy.

"We do not know how our days will be numbered when we are first born, so we have to remember that God has given us the opportunity to know love, to share love, and to be loved. And that is the most important message that I want Cindy to leave with today."

It was the varied sound of sniffles, coughing, and a few hiccups that pierced the silence whenever Pastor Craig stopped speaking. He acknowledged his audience, especially one filled with so many young teenagers. He took a deep breath and addressed them specifically.

"When we are young, we feel that every day lasts forever

and that all our tomorrows will always be there. But when we live with someone who is ill, we realize that every day is precious and there is no guarantee about tomorrow. It is very difficult to witness the dying of a loved one. But, Cindy, I need you to always remember the very best of your mom. How she held you as a baby, how she took care of you when you were sick, how she laughed with you when the two of you were silly, and how she cried with you when you were sad or discouraged."

Pastor Craig breathed in deeply giving his mourners a moment to process. He knew that people processed the written word much more quickly than the spoken one, so he made it a practice to slow down every so often for everyone to grasp his message.

He continued, "I need you to clasp the strength that your mother surrounded you with all these years. I need you to embrace her incredible love of you, the laughter she shared with you, and the tears she helped dry off of you when you were inconsolable. And most importantly, to know that your mother will always reside in your heart; she will be there every day for you and she will watch as you grow into a beautiful and smart young woman. And should the day come for you when you have your own child, your mother will be smiling, and the laughter and giggles that your baby shares with you, will be your mother's voice reminding you that she is always near."

Pastor Craig stopped here and looked around at the young teenagers and the adults. They were here to support

Cindy and he smiled with that knowledge. He knew she would have the love and friendship of everyone who surrounded her.

Pastor Craig hummed his favorite melody and then he spoke in a raspy voice, "It is not every day that I am witness to such love and support I see in front of me.

"And something that I want to say because I am not sure if everyone here knows this. One of my congregants, Neva Waverly, after some very deep and soul-reaching conversations with Muriel, has agreed to shepherd Cindy into her home. A permanent home where Cindy will grow and flourish under the tutelage, love, and care of a very special lady."

There were murmurs and nods and whispers of *Oh, my* and *that's beautiful* and *I'm so happy for her.*

Pastor Craig continued, "And now, I would like to conclude with a special celebration announcement. In memory of Muriel Newport's short but beautiful life Drs. Jeanine and Gunther Maddox and Mrs. Waverly will be hosting a remembrance of Muriel's life at the home of Neva Waverly. I hope to see all of you there following this ceremony."

Cindy took a deep breath. The realization that her teacher, the one who was always there for her from day one would be there for her from now till forever was overwhelming. She swayed and felt like fainting, but Lucas and Jáquan moved in quickly to catch her and steady her.

Lucas whispered in her ear, "Hey, Cindy, it's okay, girl, we are all here for you. And we will meet you at Mrs.

Waverly's house so don't you worry. If there is anything you need, anything at all, any one of us will be there for you. You get me?"

Cindy's eyes were closed as she still felt dizzy, but she nodded slowly.

Neva moved in and Billy was there right beside her.

Neva put her hand gently under Cindy's chin, "Hey, baby, we are going to deal with this together. Your mother will never, ever be forgotten and I will make sure of that. Now, how about all of your friends come over to my house where we can have something to eat and let today kinda sink in a bit? Yes?"

"Mrs. Waverly," Cindy asked ever so quietly, "Can I stand over by the grave a little longer? I want to stay all the way until…until…"

Neva knew what she meant. She looked over at Billy who murmured softly, "C'mon, Cindy. We will walk over with you, and we will hold onto you until you are ready to leave."

Billy shook hands with Lucas and Jáquan and then put his arm around her shoulders. Together, Billy, Neva, and Cindy walked over to where the casket was being lowered into the ground. Billy picked up the shovel by the mound of dirt and handed it to Cindy.

"Here you go, love. Now go ahead and scoop up some of the dirt and let it fall in. That's all you have to do. The rest of us will line up and we will all share in helping you say goodbye to your loving mom."

Cindy's arms felt like two bricks of heavy concrete, but she took the shovel and after digging up the dirt and tossing it in as gently as she could, she whispered through her tears, "Goodbye, Mom. I love you with all of my heart and I promise I will make you proud of me. Thank you for asking Mrs. Waverly to be my stepmother. And thank you for everything you did for me. God in heaven, watch over my mom because she is going to be your favorite angel."

And with that, Cindy handed the shovel to Billy and turned around to see everyone who had come to the funeral standing in line to participate in the ceremonial shoveling.

Billy and Neva guided Cindy to Neva's car. Before Billy left he handed Cindy an envelope. "It's from Anika and Coby and Jasmine. They weren't allowed to be here, but they wanted you to have this. I have to return to the ranch now, but when you are ready to come back before you have to start school, well, we are looking forward to having you there. We need you, Cindy. The girls need you, too." Billy hugged Cindy, then he hugged Neva and kissed her slowly on her cheek and then he was gone.

Neva grasped Cindy by her shoulders and said, "Let's go home, Cindy. We have a lot to talk about."

Cindy looked at Neva and a smile grew wide. "Thank you. Thank you. I don't know how I will ever repay you for any of this."

Neva laughed, "You already have, my dear."

CHAPTER 27

The summer flew by quickly. Everyone returned to whatever last-minute summer plans were still available. Cindy returned to working at her camp and since Neva was such good friends with Billy, it was comforting to see them together at his camp holding hands. For Cindy, being at camp meant she did not have to face the reality of losing her mom. She was looking forward to living with Neva, but it was a major change in her life and she was having an occasional panic attack whenever she thought about how her life was going to be completely different.

She would be going back to school with what she felt was a whole new identity. She wanted to talk with Miss Anna and ask her so many questions like how will Mrs. Waverly react when she is anxious or can't breathe because she is in a full-blown panic attack. Wait, she thought – what do I call her? I know in school it will be Mrs. Waverly, but if I am living with her, then what?

The more Cindy thought about the details, the more her

chest tightened. Oh, jeez, she muttered to herself, I have to get all my things from the house and move them. And my mother's belongings – what do I do with them? Do I box them up and store them? I'm not throwing them away. Cindy shook her head violently. I won't get rid of them, she swore to herself.

That night Cindy wrote a long letter to Lucas and Riley. She asked them if they could help her move everything to Mrs. Waverly's house. She hoped they could box all her mother's stuff and, she didn't know where yet, but store them – somewhere. She would figure it out soon because Mrs. Waverly had told her the house was up for sale and that whatever the house sold for Cindy would get for her college fund. So many thoughts seemed to go on endlessly in Cindy's mind.

• • •

Meanwhile, Carl and Cassandra were still enjoying their honeymoon in the Bahamas. They left right after the funeral but not before spending time at Neva's home. The married couple socialized with everyone, and when they felt they had spent the appropriate time they slipped away without anyone noticing that they had left. Well, Neva noticed; she just smiled to herself while she was cleaning up the mound of dishes in her kitchen.

• • •

Lila made it a special point to attend the celebration at Neva's house. These were important relationships with her students and Lila was well aware of how tragedy affected her students. Lila spent a few moments chatting with everyone, especially Cindy, and then, after looking at her watch, announced softly to herself, *Well, I better be going home now. I have some issues I need to fix.*

The earlier conversation with her son, Benjamin, was not a successful one. It had been over a week since Meadow was released from the hospital. Ben tried texting her but Meadow was not answering him. Ben was not allowed to visit her according to Meadow's parents. Not now. Maybe not ever.

Lila and her husband, Darrius, were sitting in their living room staring at their son. They had spoken to him the day of Meadow's miscarriage, but that day was too volatile to have any kind of serious let alone a calm conversation. They gave Ben time. They needed time to collect their own thoughts on what to say to Ben regarding Meadow's miscarriage.

"Ben," began Darrius, "I thought you and I had that special talk quite a while ago. Yes?"

Ben fidgeted in his hair, his long legs twitching back and forth while his large hands grabbed handfuls of his soft curly hair.

"Mmmm, yeah, I remember."

"Excuse me?"

Ben sat up, his light hazel eyes blurred under threatening tears but he was too proud to let them fall.

"I said, yes sir, Dad," murmured Ben.

Lila could not stand his insolence a second longer. She

clapped her hands together to get his attention and spat out, "How dare you disrespect us like this? After all we have done for you? After all we have given you!"

Darrius did not want to go down that path. It was the old guilt trip, and he did not want to add that negativity to the conversation.

Darrius cleared his throat. "Son, are you aware, no, really and truly aware of what just happened? Son, your life…your life as you know it was about to be changed forever." Darrius choked on the last few words and he had to cough before he could continue.

But Lila was not having it. She stood up, her gray eyes turning a dark steely color that deepened with every word she spoke.

"Son. . .Benjamin, I'll say it again. Where was the respect for Meadow? How many times have I lectured you with my own mother's saying that when the big head tells the little head what to do you are in deep shit! Seriously, Benny…"

Ben stood up next to his mother and she realized that at sixteen years old he was taller than she was and she was a tall woman.

"Mom, I love Meadow. I want to be with her always. And, well, dammit, if she had not had gone and lost the baby…"

"She didn't lose the baby, Ben," Lila corrected angrily, "She suffered a miscarriage, and that is extremely traumatic for any woman regardless of her age."

"Fine," argued Ben becoming defiant, "so it's called a miscarriage. And I will be with her while she recovers and had she not los…had she not had a miscarriage, I would have been with her and Mom… Dad…I would have married her, too. I want to be with her forever. Just like the two of you."

"Oh, no you don't," jumped in Darrius, "you don't get to play that game, Son. Do not compare yourself to your mother and me…uh no…no sir. At your age, I was playing basketball and dating three different women and having a blast. I was not getting ready to have a baby! I wanted to go to college and travel and not settle down.

"And, more importantly, I used protection. Protection, Son. That is the key word here. And it was a major part of our father and son conversation that you obviously did not recall."

Ben argued vehemently, "I remembered every word, Dad, but, well, I didn't have money to buy the protection because someone in this room held my allowance for the last few months just because I forgot to do my damn chores."

"You will not curse in this house, young man," Lila interrupted, growing impatient with his flippant attitude. "And completing chores and demonstrating responsibility as a member of this household does not dictate any monetary compensation. And had you gone to your father and asked him for his help in this matter, he would have gladly come to your aid even if he was not in agreement with the purpose of it!"

"Okay," Darrius said softly, "we are not getting anything resolved this way. Your mother and I will be meeting with Meadow's parents later this evening and we will be having an adult conversation regarding the future of the two of you should they even allow you to continue seeing Meadow."

"They can't stop me!" Ben shouted, his hands balled into fists and swinging recklessly in the air.

Suddenly Bessie opened the front door, her long brown hair sashaying across her back, "Hello, Parental Units. I'm back. What's up? Everyone happy in here?"

Ben stared at her and spit out, "Go away, you brat. Can't you see we are busy here!"

Lila took one step closer to Ben until her nose was almost touching his chin. "You need to dial it back right now and remember where you are and who you are. That is your sister who idolizes you and thinks the sun rises and sets by your schedule – so watch your mouth.

"I think our conversation is over now. Darrius, do you agree? Ben, you need to go to your room and reflect on today's discussion. We will continue this talk at another time."

Bessie, clueless about everything that just transpired, shrugged her shoulders and went into the kitchen looking for a snack.

Ben, defeated and depressed, turned and trudged to his bedroom.

Darrius and Lila, overcome with the emotions of the day, grabbed each other and stayed there for quite some time in an embrace that strengthened them, but only temporarily.

CHAPTER 28

It was a teacher's cliché, but the summer turned cold and ended all too soon as it always did when you were young and especially when you were a teacher. The school was abuzz with new students, new staff, new schedules, and a new excitement and anticipation with all that comes with a new school year.

Cindy felt a bit awkward knowing that everyone recognized that Neva was not only her teacher but also her guardian. Cindy was still struggling with a title. Would she eventually call her Mom? Stepmom? Neva? Cindy had mixed feelings, but for now, she felt a huge weight had been lifted. Her mother's house, small though it was, was on the market and whatever profit was to be made for the house, Neva had told her that the income from the sale would go directly into her college fund. In addition, Neva had meticulously gone over all the paperwork her mom had shared including a trust fund that had been set up for her with the sad understanding that she was not going to be there for her daughter. It made Cindy cry every time she thought about her mom, laying there in her hospice bed thinking about who was going to take care of her daughter.

Mattie would never leave Cindy to fend for herself. The thought of her daughter being an orphan strangled her thoughts daily. There were no relatives, no friends that Mattie could ever imagine leaving her Cindy with except… She knew Cindy thought the world of Neva, so it came as no surprise for Mattie to contact Neva. It was a huge undertaking, an incredible responsibility, and possibly a massive burden. Mattie would have understood if Neva had politely declined but thank God she agreed and with such an open heart. And when Neva shared her own story of when she lost her baby, well, Mattie bonded and knew she had made the right decision. Women sharing poignant and intimate heartbreaking stories, maybe that was a cliché, but it was definitely the glue.

Cindy's friends knew about her new situation, and they embraced her and never made her feel awkward.

Riley, of course, was the first to find Cindy that morning before homeroom.

"Hey, hey, girl," laughed Riley. "So, now you've got an in with a teacher, I may be asking you for a preview of our first test. You got me? Besides, after working at the barbeque company all summer, my cooking skills are over the top. You and I could, well, ya know, trade food for inside info!"

Cindy smiled, "Oh, yeah, for sure. I'm gonna go through her desk drawers and pull out the quizzes and tests and just pass them around. Maybe I'll even charge so I can start saving for a car. Waddya think?"

Riley cackled in a wicked way, "I think I like the new you, CinCin!!"

Jilly came running down the hall, breathless and smiling and Riley thought she was giggling.

Riley grabbed her before she ran into Cindy. "What's happening, Jilly?"

Jilly couldn't stop laughing. "I can't wait till lunch. I think something very exciting is going to happen and I can't stop cracking myself up."

Cindy looked at her with her gorgeous green eyes and her long blonde hair and wished one day she could look that beautiful.

Cindy asked tentatively because she was not that close a friend with Jilly, "Uhh, Jilly, what's going to happen at lunch today? Are we going to have a fire drill?"

Jilly scrunched her nose and closed her eyes. Cindy was such a geek, thought Jilly, but she did feel sorry for her so she said as sincerely as she could, "I heard through a few friends that Lucas might want to talk to me…again."

Cindy gasped. "You mean, you would… I mean after what happened last year… I mean, no I'm sorry, that's not for me to say…I…"

Riley bounced right in, "Look, Jilly, if you like Lucas, and I mean more than just because he is the school's football hero and a stud to look at, well, you better make sure he knows you have limits and all. Right? You do, don't you? Cause you know what can happen just because he thinks he can, you know what I mean."

Cindy looked confused and dazed. She had worked with Lucas and Riley when they helped move all her things from her old house to Mrs. Waverly's house. She thought Lucas was the sweetest and kindest boy she had ever met. When Riley was not in earshot, Lucas even brought up Miss Anna and how much he liked talking to her about his issues. Not that Cindy would ever ask Lucas what those issues were, but she thought it was super cool that he talked to her about something personal.

Riley turned to Cindy's bewildered face and whispered, "I'll explain later, okay? Meantime, just listen, alright?"

The school bell rang notifying everyone to go to homeroom. The three girls looked at each other, Riley high-fived Jilly and then turning to Cindy urged her with, "Go on, Cindy. Everyone knows what's going on with you. You don't have to look around and be nervous. And for God's sake, no panic attacks. This is your new normal. Get used to it. Go!"

The girls each turned and ran to their new homerooms.

Lucas sat in his homeroom and looked around. The guys: Jáquan, Aiden, Roland, Mateo, and Tommy all nodded in agreement.

Lucas took a slow, deep breath and then raised his hand.

Carl DeWitt sighed. This wasn't going to be easy he thought. But he would deal. And he would be okay with it.

"Yes, Lucas? What's up, man?"

"So, Mr. D., like the fellas and all, well, we heard you were pretty busy this summer, huh?"

There were snickers and guffaws and a few throats were cleared. Even some of the girls giggled.

"So, Mr. D., like is it true?"

Carl smiled. He loved teaching. He loved kids. And what's more, he loved joking with them because it was so easy. "Well, Lucas, yes, it's true. I went on a special vacation." Carl could not help laughing out loud.

Lucas grinned. "Duh, Mr. D. Like more than just a vacation. We heard you went with someone. You know, someone special. We all knew it. We did. But everyone here is too chicken to ask you." Lucas turned around to all the guys and shrugged his shoulders waiting for them to pipe in agreement, but they shuffled their feet and pretended to look around the room.

Now it was Carl's turn. "Too chicken to ask me? You gotta be kidding. I can't wait to share the great news with all of you. It's true. It's true. I am going to be in the next Marvel movie. I spent the entire summer in California auditioning and I was so surprised when they called me and…"

Lucas stood up. "Hey, wait a minute. That's not what we thought. Nah, you lying, Mr. D. Now tell us true."

Carl waited and waited. He looked over at the anxious faces just dying to hear what they all think happened. They loved their gossip ring and they needed to find out the real truth.

Carl could not hold back any longer. Their anxious faces looked back at him like they were going to burst. He laughed long and hard and finally, he said, "Yes, my peeps. It is true. I married the very beautiful Miss Conway who you will now all address as Mrs. DeWitt."

The room exploded in cheers and clapping and lots of 'whooo hooos' and congratulations.

"Okay, now that we are all clear here about how I spent my summer vacation, it's time to move on to the real business of homeroom. I need to hand out your schedules and, hey, no whining."

Homeroom lasted an hour and then as soon as the bell rang everyone scattered.

The halls were filled with students rushing to find their next classes, to catch up with their friends to see who was in class with whom, and where to meet when the lunch bell rang.

Neva, as always, stood outside of her room watching and looking to see if anyone needed help. She spotted Cindy walking down the hall. Their eyes met and the smiles on both of their faces spoke volumes. Neva thought to herself, this is not the same Cindy I helped off the floor a year ago. Neva raised her arm and called out, "Have a great day, Sweetheart. See you later on."

Cindy could not stop smiling. She waved back and entered the classroom down the hall. She had never felt more calm in her life. It was going to be a great school year.

CHAPTER 29

Lila sat in her office. She knew she needed to go out into the halls, but she wanted to take a moment by herself. Her son was growing up and she and her husband were taking the time to talk with him every night about his goals, his life, and his relationship with Meadow. Meadow's parents had met with Lila and Darrius and after a long conversation about their children, came to realize that restricting them from seeing each other would only cause them to see each other in secret. They did not want that to happen. They wanted transparency and honesty and most importantly, they needed to trust one another. Dealing with over two thousand teenagers every day in the building was truly much easier than dealing with one teenager at home.

Jeff Stineman knocked at her door. "Hi, boss. How you doing today? Wanna walk down to the cafeteria? It's time."

Lila looked up from her desk. Jeff Stineman had suffered a mild heart attack over the summer and since then he had been making sure he was following his nutritionist's advice which included an increase in his physical activities.

Lila stood up. "Hey there, Mr. Stineman. You are looking good, my man. What, have you lost now how much? Ten, twenty?"

Jeff smiled. "I want you to know that as of this morning, I have lost over thirty-five pounds and still going strong. It doesn't hurt that I patrol the halls a zillion times a day."

Lila smiled. Just as she exited her office, Barbara Atkinson walked out of her office. "Okay, time for cafeteria duty. I'm on it." Barbara had a hard time smiling because she felt her job was too serious for jocularity. Besides, knowing that some of the teachers still called her BA behind her back did not make her feel all warm and fuzzy. I can't help it, she rationalized, if being called 'Battle Axe" just because I am allworkeveryday is the reason, well, so be it.

The power pack threesome walked by Cassandra's desk. "Why, good day, Mrs. DeWitt," said Lila with a huge grin on her face. Cassandra blushed from her neck all the way up to her forehead. She wasn't used to being called Mrs. anything let alone being married to a teacher in the building.

On her first day back, both Amelia Goddard and Joanne Cumberly had come running out of the main office to greet her with flowers and a few wedding gifts that they could not wait for her to open. The three of them ruled the main office and it was a joyful reunion not to mention hearing Cassandra squeal and giggle at the beautiful wedding gifts they showered upon her.

"Hello to you," returned Cassandra. "Oh, and Gloria Lomack is looking for…well, I guess for all of you at the moment."

Barbara rolled her eyes and Jeff covered his mouth while fake coughing and Lila looked at both of them with her *don't you dare laugh or say anything unprofessional – both of you!*

And just like that Gloria, in all her glory, came running down the hall towards them. Well, one could not really call that running, more like fast shuffling. At any rate, there was Gloria, huffing and puffing.

"Oh, gosh. Oh, my. I……am…so glad I caught up… oh, I need to catch my breath."

Lila spoke for the group, "It's okay, Gloria. We are all here now. Take a moment to breathe, my dear, and then let us know what in the world is causing you to run down to us like this."

Jeff could not hold back. "Did the soda machine break down again?"

It took all she could to not burst out laughing, but Barbara controlled herself. She smiled and Jeff thought she might crack her cheek, but he knew he would have been elbowed in his gut had he joked about that to Barbara.

Barbara cleared her throat. "So, Gloria. Is anyone hurt? Do we need to call an ambulance? Or the fire department? You have all of our attention so, please, clue us in. And quickly, too. We have to be in the cafeteria because it's almost lunch time and this place will be like the mall on steroids."

"Well," Gloria began feeling quite important. "You are not going to believe your ears. Get ready for the hottest piece of student info on the market today."

Lila was getting impatient and started walking away towards the cafeteria.

"Wait!" begged Gloria. "Here it is."

All the administrators turned and looked at Gloria with that look. That look that said *you better tell us now 'cause we have important things to do!*

"Okay, okay. Here it is. Do you know we have two sophomores who are cousins, right?"

Barbara jumped in. "Of course, Shaynee Moulder and Stetson Roscoe. So?"

Gloria could not contain herself. "Do you know that Ms. Raizel Glenstone…"

Jeff wanted to be included so he interrupted, "Our Physical Education/Health teacher?"

Gloria was poised and ready to pounce. "Yes! Yes! Well, she had come to see me at the end of the year to let me know that Shaynee had been talking to her about some very personal items regarding…uhh…what did she call it?"

Lila came up to Gloria and put her arms around her. "How about we walk and talk, my dear, because lunch will be here and gone before you can finish your most interesting information."

Gloria nodded and now the four of them paraded down the hall all the while with Gloria, her hands punching the air with every sentence she spoke, and her New York accent getting thicker with each punctuation.

"Yes," urged Lila. "Go on, Gloria. We are almost out of time."

Gloria took a deep breath. "Yes, Lila. Yes…okay. So Shaynee's mom just called me to let me know that both Shaynee AND Stetson will not be in school for about another two weeks."

Barbara and Jeff both said at the same time, "Why not?"

Gloria smiled. A huge smile just like the Cheshire Cat and she was enjoying every second of holding back and then she burst out, "Because the two of them are NOT cousins. Holy shit, guess what?! The two of them are twins! And their father, who happens to live in Puerto Rico, just invited them down to visit and meet all of their other family there! And that's why they will be late joining us for the school year! Oh, and I cannot wait to hear how this family is going to deal with this juicy drama! Yep, you gotta love school shit, oops, I mean family relationships and stuff. " Gloria turned around and laughing, skipped down the hall to her counseling office.

• • •

The bell rang and the student body poured out of their classes like a washing machine overflowing with suds. Everyone was rushing to meet friends, go to their lockers, and race to the cafeteria to eat as much as they could before their next class.

Jilly found Riley and Cindy and Whitney and Sondra

and Lane. She couldn't wait to sit and talk about the day so far.

The girls were all busy chatting and gossiping and giggling when Jáquan and Tommy and Mateo came up to their table.

"Uhhh," began Jáquan, "Hey, Jilly, you gotta second?"

The girls all chuckled and urged Jilly on. "You go, Jilly," said Riley, "See if the boys can talk in real sentences. See what they want."

Jilly stood up and gave the girls that *okay, let it go* look.

This time Tommy spoke up. "Hey, Jilly, ummmmm, see…like…"

Riley laughed hard and loud. "Really, guys, can't any of you form a few words that might make any sense?"

Mateo jumped in, "Okay, it's like this…Jilly…girl… Lucas.."

Lane interrupted, "Lucas? Where is he? Why isn't he with you?"

"Jeez, guys, I'm trying to tell ya," begged Mateo. "Okay, I'm saying it right out. Jilly, Lucas wants to go to Homecoming with you, but he's too damned scared to ask you because of…because of…well you remember last year."

Jilly turned bright red with the stinging memory of her encounter with Lucas in that dark dead end of a hallway. And the punishment, the embarrassment, the scorn she felt afterward for so long.

Jilly looked at the guys. "You tell Lucas that if he wants to ask me out, he's going to have to pull up his big boy football pants and ask me himself."

Riley clapped followed by all the girls on the table with a few yeahs and whooo hooos to follow.

The boys, their shoulders slumped in unison, turned around and went to find their tables.

The lunch period was over and everyone was walking out of the cafeteria. Jilly felt someone tug at her shoulder and turned around to see Lucas, his deep blue eyes staring right at her. She felt her heart flutter. Why does my heart always feel like a runaway butterfly when Lucas is near me she said to herself shaking her head as though that would stop the funny feeling.

Lucas stumbled at first, but then he gained a bit more confidence. "Hey, Jilly. I'm so very sorry about last year. I promise I won't do anything stupid, ever. And, hey, would you like to go to homecoming with me this year? My step-dad, we're cool now, he'll drive us and all and…"

Jilly smiled, put her hand on Lucas's shoulder, and said softly, "I'd love to, Lucas."

CHAPTER 30

Beverly sat in her car. She was munching on carrots and a piece of cheese. It was too early to walk into the building. Another school year. Damn it all. Another school.

"I don't give a shit where I teach," she said out loud to herself. "If I never have to see that Dr. Carter again I will be happy for the rest of my life." Beverly laughed to herself, a haunting malicious sound that erupted from deep inside of her. I wonder how many times poor Lillian, that wimp of a secretary, had to go sit on the potty. Giving her a box of chocolates laced with Exlax was the best going-away present I could ever have created! God, I'm good!

Beverly, having been released to the custody of her mother, had regained her teaching position with the understanding that she would not be going back to Wells. She didn't care. A school was a school and kids were kids. She liked teaching. She liked her content. It was the other teachers who bothered her. They were indignant. They were a bunch of pompous, know-it-alls. Beverly did not like them and they did not appreciate her esteemed teaching strategies.

She was told, in her special "return to school" meeting that if she had any more incidents like the one at Wells, she would be terminated. This was her last chance. She didn't care. She would just be more careful this time.

Beverly observed the large number of cars entering the parking lot. She squinted her beady eyes as she watched them park their cars, and grab their satchels along with brand new rolling suitcases filled with all kinds of teaching "stuff" as they marched proudly and excitedly into the building for their first day.

And then she saw him. She knew his name because she was introduced to him at the preservice meetings. His name was, damn, what was it? Her fingers drummed on the steering wheel and then it came to her. Louis. Louis Spears. Yes. All the teachers loved Louis. The male teachers, the female teachers. I suppose the students all loved him, too.

Beverly snickered and said with a sinister smirk as she got out of her car, "Oh, Louis. Why, my, my…look how everyone likes you, or shall I add they must all adore you. Hmmmm, I guess I might have to let a few important people in the main office know about your afternoon private meetings with a few of your students. Your male students." And then she burst out a laugh, a long, diabolical laugh. A few of the teachers turned around when they heard the laugh, which to those who heard it, did not sound normal or happy at all.

Beverly looked at them, smiled, and said as sweetly as she could without poisoning her tone, "Why, good morning, everyone. I'm so happy to be here. I can't wait for the school year to get started!"

ACKNOWLEDGMENTS

- Ilene Tockman – you have truly been my guardian angel as you supported, guided, and embraced my works. I love that you were always ready and willing to read each chapter pushing me to continue and to not give up. My love and appreciation to you forever!
- Daniel Rose – Since you were an infant (and before!) I have shared my love of reading with you. How beautiful it is that you have developed your passion for reading and writing. And now, what an honor for me to have you as the editor of my books! Keep reading…keep writing…and please keep editing for me. I love you, my son.
- Mark Rose – You are my soul and the light of my life. Thank you for helping me put out fires – daily- and never giving up on me especially when those doors get slammed. Together we have built a life filled with love, children, and grandchildren. I love you for that and so much more.
- Debbie Bernhardt -I loved visiting your horse farm and learning so much from you about

your horses. Thank you for allowing me to walk around in my happy place for being surrounded by horses has a very special meaning to me.

- Shae McMullin – Thank you very much for working with me on the cover. It is not every day that I get to share my vision with someone who completely understands what I want in a cover. Your creativity and design were spot on and I appreciate all the time you spent with me.

- Kerry – Thank you, Kerry, for your critique of the book. Your big picture was exactly what I needed to frame the book and develop the closure necessary.

- Lisa Gilliam– Thank you, Lisa, for making sure my interior design was top-notch – and it was. I appreciate all the hard work you did for me.

- Victoria Griffin – I have enjoyed working with you on these last two books and I hope to continue our partnership with my next two. Your professionalism along with the support of your fabulous team have been extremely supportive and positive every step of the way. Thank you from the bottom of my heart.

www.ingramcontent.com/pod-product-compliance
Lightning Source LLC
Chambersburg PA
CBHW061529310726
48972CB00008B/2375